Seeking Serenity

A Heartwarming Women's Fiction Novel

The Mended Hearts Ranch
Book 1

Casey Edwards

Prologue

Gus Simpson

The man watched his hired hands as they laughed and blew off steam at the bar. From where he was sitting in a back booth, it was obvious they didn't know their boss was watching them. The bartender, Cassie, was the only one who seemed aware of his existence.

She glanced his way, almost as if she were drawn by his thoughts, checking to see if he needed a refill on his beer. He shook his head slightly, and she beamed a beautiful smile before looking away.

He took a sip of his beer, remembering his youth as he watched the men at the bar. He'd been at the top of his game back then, one of the top bull riders on the circuit, destined, some said, to win the national championship. That all changed that Friday night when he got on that rank bull owned by Josh Windham. His name was Destroyer, and no one knew at the time how apt that name would be. He certainly didn't.

And that's exactly what that bull did. It only took a little under eight seconds for that bull to destroy his life as he knew it. The bull wasn't content with tossing him to the ground like a sack of taters. No, he had to do one better than that. Destroyer stomped him into the dirt, breaking dang near every bone in his body. There was no way he'd ever ride a bull again after taking that much damage. All of his dreams were gone in an instant.

He'd never forget waking up in the hospital weeks later, alone. They said it was a miracle he was alive, but at the time, it didn't feel like one. All he could think about was everything he'd lost.

A few weeks before the accident, riding high on a wave of success, he'd done something stupid. Something unforgivable. He'd been drinking in the bar with his buddies when a gorgeous woman walked in. All thoughts of his long-time girlfriend, Rose, had flown out of his head when he saw that woman. He'd taken her back to his hotel, and Rose walked right in on them. He could still remember the shock and hurt on her face when she saw them.

Five years of love, gone in an instant. They'd planned on getting married that year after he won the national championship. Rose had reached out to him when he was in the hospital, but he ignored her, preferring to wallow in his guilt. He snorted and took another sip, reminding himself it was what he deserved. He'd picked his path, and it was his job to walk it, no matter how many regrets blocked it. After all, would he be here now if things had been different? Knowing who he'd been back then? Probably not.

But these young cowboys who worked on his new ranch? They were different. They had their whole lives ahead of them. Right now, they were untrained young bucks who were determined to live life to the fullest. They'd most likely left a slew of broken hearts behind them. The love of a good woman could move mountains, and he was betting their lives were all about to change.

At first, he'd intended his ranch to help its future guests, but the more he got to know the men who worked for him, the more convinced he became that they could use some help, too.

He spotted Cassie looking at Jack Waters with calf eyes while he high-fived Doc at the bar. She must have felt Gus looking at her, and their eyes met through the shadows. She tossed the bar towel over her shoulder and filled up a glass, skirting around the bar and heading in his direction.

Instead of just replacing the glass, as he'd expected, she slid it in front of him and took a seat on the other side of the booth. Her smile lit up the dark space like a beacon.

"Here you go, Mr. Simpson," she said with a cheeky grin.

His head snapped back. He didn't know how she knew his real name. He hadn't come in here much since he'd bought the ranch, preferring to keep to himself. Sure, he'd known this was a small town and news traveled faster than a wildfire after a ten-year drought, but he thought he'd kept his real identity a secret. It had been long enough; surely they wouldn't remember an old bull rider who'd disappeared off the circuit.

"How do you know my name?"

She grinned again and took the towel off her shoulder, wiping at an imaginary spot on the table. Cassie ran a clean place, one of the nicest bars he'd ever seen.

"As if I wouldn't recognize Gus Simpson, one of the world's best bull riders. My daddy was your biggest fan. He still plays your old rides on his VHS machine. One of these days, I'm gonna digitize them and surprise him with some new DVDs."

He looked around the crowded bar, nervously licking his lips. The last thing he wanted was for word to get out about who he really was. As far as they knew, he was a rich eccentric who wanted to play at being a big-time rancher. They didn't need to know the truth.

"Cassie, I'd appreciate it if you kept that quiet. Round these parts, I've been going by Jim Bohannon."

She gave him a brisk nod, and her eyes twinkled.

"You got it, Mr. Simpson, I mean, Mr. Bohannon. Your secret's safe with me. What made you buy the old Rainey place, anyway? I'd figure with your investment experience you'd be living the high life someplace exotic."

"You know that about me, too?"

"Like I said, my daddy thinks the sun rises and sets on you. He showed me this article he'd read a few years ago. If he only knew you were here, I don't know what he'd do."

He looked around again, feeling the need to escape

as panic clawed at his throat. Her soft hand on his arm startled him. He stared down at it, not understanding.

"I won't tell a soul. I promise. I just remembered him talking about how proud he was of your accomplishments. You took your prize money and invested it instead of blowing it after the... well, after the accident. You were one of the first people to believe in cryptocurrency, for Pete's sake. That's just amazing."

He relaxed, leaning back into the booth with a chuckle.

"Call me Gus. Anyone around here who knows about crypto deserves to call me by my real name. To answer your other question, I bought the Rainey place because I've got some plans. Big plans."

He nodded his head toward the bar, where his cowboys were getting louder. The tallest, Kade, was banging his glass on the bar and looking around for Cassie.

"I'm coming," she said, trying to be heard above the noise. "Hold your dang horses. I'll be right back, Gus."

She gave him a nod as she slid out of the booth and took care of the thirsty cowboys. She was a marvel to watch, efficient as all get-out and friendly without being too friendly. He noticed Jack sneaking a few glances at her and smiled briefly. His turn would come.

Cassie was right. He'd made some smart investments. They'd paid off better than he'd ever dreamed they could. Forbes had him listed as one of the world's top billionaires, for whatever that was worth. All that money hadn't bought him any happiness, but maybe it could buy these young folks a little slice of it. He nodded as the final phases of his plans clicked into place in his head.

"Sorry about that, Gus," Cassie said, interrupting his thoughts as she sat back down across from him. "So, what do you plan to do with the Rainey place now? I'd heard it was pretty run-down."

He nodded, taking another sip and trying not to wince in front of her. She gave him an encouraging smile.

"The plan is to turn the place into one of the finest guest ranches in the state. We've got the main house with the luxury suites finished. The bunkhouse is done, and then we'll start working on phase two, building cabins. The land was what I wanted."

And land was what he'd gotten. Over half a million acres of good Wyoming pasture, with plenty of lakes and creeks. It was practically paradise for an old cowboy like him. He'd hired the ten men currently whooping it up at the bar to help him build his dream. Each one had been carefully selected, even if they weren't aware of it. A few were locals, like Jack and Austin, but the rest had come from Montana, Colorado, and even one from California. All that was left was to put the rest of his plan in motion.

"Are you gonna change the name?" Cassie asked, bringing him back to the present.

"Already have. Even got my new brand registered. It's now The Mended Hearts Ranch."

"I love that name," she said with a sigh. "What made you pick it?"

He bit back a chuckle and nodded his head back

toward the bar. He pulled his wallet out and handed her a fifty.

"Looks like the boys are getting restless. I've got to be going."

"Gus, this is too much. Let me go get you some change."

"Keep it, Cassie. Have a good night. Remember, don't tell anyone about me."

She nodded before bustling back to the bar, waving at the boys to quiet down while she filled their drink orders. He paused in the doorway, confident it was dark enough he wouldn't be spotted. If Cassie knew who he was, chances were there were others around here who might, too. He frowned as he watched Tex clown around at the bar. He was going to be a difficult one. In fact, out of the ten men he'd hired, he was the one who reminded him most of himself. He shook his head as he walked out of the bar and headed for his pickup.

Gus fired up the old engine and steered for the ranch, rolling the windows down so he could enjoy the crisp night air. The seasons were just changing to spring, and the promise of warmer days was just over the horizon. He massaged his left arm as he drove, the aching bones letting him know bad weather was coming.

The ranch yard was deserted, but there was a light on over the window at the kitchen sink. The house was enormous, a relic of the past, when ranchers had large families and needed space for as many kids as they could turn out. It would serve as the start-up for his new business. While he knew some would prefer the peace of a little cabin, he thought city folks would appreciate a few of the finer things in life, even if they were in the middle of nowhere.

He shuffled up the steps and winced, lifting his face to the sky. It was too warm for snow, so that must mean rain was coming. He shouldered in through the door and hung his hat on the hook.

"You were out later than I thought you'd be," a soft voice said from the hall.

"Martha, you didn't need to wait up for me," Gus said, shrugging out of his coat.

"I worry about you, sir. Can I get you anything before you turn in? Some tea for your bones?"

Martha was his housekeeper, and she'd been with him for over fifteen years. Her skills as a cook were going to enable the ranch to gain a reputation as a real guest ranch. She never said much, but she always knew when he was hurting. The woman made the most fantastic herbal teas that were guaranteed to make pain a distant memory. He nodded as he shuffled toward his suite.

"If you wouldn't mind."

"Not at all. I've already got the water brewing."

He slowly eased himself into the chair in the corner of his room. Gus glanced out the window, seeing the shape of the bunkhouse silhouetted by the rising moon. It had gone up quickly, thanks to some local carpenters who appreciated the extra money he'd tossed in as motivation. All that remained were a few finishing touches on the inside.

Martha came into the room and placed the tea on the table. She gave him a quick nod and turned to leave.

"Good night, sir. Your breakfast will be ready by six."

"Thanks, Martha."

She closed the door behind her, and he turned off the lamp, letting the moon serve as his light. So far, all of his plans had come together nicely. All that remained was to put the rest of them in motion. He picked up the journal he kept on the table and paged through it to his list of their names. Who would be first?

He shook his head as he tried to decide. Jack, the local cowboy who was the perfect match for Cassie? No, they weren't quite ready yet. There was history there, and he knew it would take a herculean effort to help those two. He took a drink of his tea, draining the cup. That meant Austin would be his first pick. The handsome cowboy was just about to turn thirty and had shown no signs he was ready to settle down. Gus knew from experience that could change in an instant if he met the right woman.

He turned the page and made a note next to Austin's name. He had the perfect woman in mind for him. In the morning, he'd call a friend who ran a travel magazine in Los Angeles and put things into motion. With any luck, some money, and a little intervention, he could set these cowboys, who reminded him so much of himself, on a path to love and happiness. He closed his eyes and sent up a prayer.

"Dear God in Heaven, please help me make a difference in these young people's lives. You said that to those who are given much, much is expected. Well, you've certainly blessed me with more money than I could ever spend. I'm here to do my part and right some old wrongs. I've never asked for anything for myself, but please, work through me."

He bowed his head in a silent amen. Rose filled his thoughts as he hobbled over to the bed, excited about the future for the first time in a long time. He'd drifted for years before settling on this plan. He knew he might not right the wrongs that plagued his life, but he could make a difference in the lives of these ten young men and ten young women. Tomorrow was the start of something special.

Chapter One

Serenity

Some people enjoy flying, rocketing toward their destination at a couple hundred miles an hour, with hardly a thought about it. Serenity Adams was not one of them. She gripped the armrest hard as the plane descended, desperate to think of anything but the fact that she was hurtling toward the earth in a big metal tube, with only a fragile set of landing gear to break the fall.

She glanced out the window, craning her head to see around the sleeping form of the man in the window seat. She got a quick glimpse of white-peaked mountains before the plane lurched, taking her stomach with it. She closed her eyes and breathed through her nose.

You'd think a travel writer, known for jet-setting and covering exotic locations, wouldn't have any problem with flight. Serenity's lip quirked slightly, and she shook her head as she counted her breaths. She'd gotten somewhat used to the bigger transatlantic planes, but this puddle jumper was a whole other story. When she'd boarded the tiny plane in Denver to head to a remote corner of Wyoming, she wasn't sure what exactly she'd expected, but it wasn't this.

Had she gone temporarily insane when she agreed to cover this story? Her boss, Herman Thompson, was a hard man to say no to. He'd been her editor for the past ten years and had taught her everything she knew about reporting. When he'd asked her, as a personal favor, to visit one of his friends' ranches in Wyoming, she couldn't really say no.

So here she was, heading to a tiny town in the Wyoming wilderness, to cover a brand new luxury guest ranch. A ranch, of all things. It was a far cry from the spectacular retreats in Fiji and Ibiza she'd grown accustomed to. So far, her experience with cowboys was limited to a few television shows and movies.

Her mind drifted to the fight she'd had with her boyfriend the night before. They shared an apartment in Los Angeles, and even though they'd spent little time together over the past year, she'd thought they'd just focused on their jobs. Living the lives of busy young professionals set on making their way in the world together. Maybe she'd been wrong. From the way Chad had rolled his eyes and snapped at her when she'd told him about her next assignment, she had a sneaking suspicion something else was going on.

Even though she knew it was pointless, she glanced

at her phone, hoping he'd answered one of the many texts she'd sent while waiting in the airport for her connecting flight. Nope, still nothing.

Chasing that thought away, she focused on the brief Herm had given her before she'd left. It was short, and she'd practically memorized it. A friend of his, Jim Bohannon, had set up a new guest ranch, but it wasn't your typical dude ranch. Whatever that was. Her experience with dude ranches was limited to that movie with Billy Crystal.

Instead of wowing city folks with horseback rides and the chance to play at being cowboys, this place was set up to help the heartbroken heal and find hope again. She was so intrigued that she would've taken the assignment even if old Herm hadn't asked for it as a favor.

The engines whined as she let out another slow breath and cracked her eyes. Her seatmate was still sleeping, even as the plane bounced hard and swerved to the right. How on earth could someone sleep through a landing? The pilot's voice crackled through the intercom, and the man next to her finally stirred, giving her a small smile as he tucked his travel pillow away into his bag.

She shoved her feet into her heels and grabbed her purse, thankful she'd checked her carry-on instead of lugging it through three airports. The other passengers crowded into the aisle, and she felt a whiff of air go past her head as someone swung their bag down a little too close. She glanced over her shoulder, and the woman gave her the universal "sorry" expression before turning to her husband.

Serenity tucked her hair behind her ear, practicing patience as the rest of the rows behind her filtered toward the front. At least with a small plane, you didn't have to wait as long, she thought as she finally stood and made her way down the cramped space. She nodded to the flight attendants and turned to exit the plane, stopping short when she realized she was standing outside.

Instead of the typical gate setup, there was a metal staircase leading down to the tarmac. Well, this was different, she thought as she headed down the rickety steps, praying she wouldn't get a heel stuck. Once her feet were safely on the pavement, she glanced up, breath catching in her throat as she spotted the mountains to the west.

As a girl who'd grown up near Sacramento, she'd dreamed of working in the big city and traveling to exotic locations. That had been the driving force behind her choosing a career as a travel writer. Even though she'd seen some of the world's best beaches and the towering peaks of the Alps, there was something special, something unexpected, about the mountains of Wyoming.

The clear blue sky was so vibrant, it almost felt like she'd wandered onto a movie set and was staring at a green screen. The fluffy white clouds looked almost like they'd been drawn onto the canvas of the sky. The air hit her lungs, feeling almost crispy somehow as it passed through her nose. She definitely wasn't in L.A. anymore. A man prodded her gently in the back, and she came back to herself, feeling silly for getting caught gawking.

She hustled after the other passengers and headed toward the terminal.

She took one last lingering look at the snowy peaks before heading inside. Her phone started vibrating in her bag, startling her out of her thoughts. She slipped it out of its pocket and frowned as she saw the list of notifications. The one person she'd been hoping would write hadn't. Maybe he'd call later, or text, or something. She sighed as she put her phone back, determined to deal with everything later. Her heels clicked on the tile floor as she headed toward the baggage claim area with a few other passengers.

The carousel was creaking along slowly, and it felt like an eternity before she spotted her simple black bag. She winced as she heaved it onto the floor. As usual, she'd over-packed. She was due to spend a week at the ranch, and she knew she'd probably only use half of what she brought, but somehow, it felt better being prepared.

As she cruised toward the exit, Serenity spotted a store selling western gear. Her eyes lingered on the fringed shirts and hats that were nearly bigger than she was. A pair of turquoise-colored cowboy boots caught her eye, and she smiled, glancing ruefully down at her heels. Maybe she wasn't that prepared after all.

Serenity shrugged and forced her feet to keep moving. Herm said that the ranch was sending a driver, but as she glanced around the lobby of the airport, she didn't see anyone besides her fellow passengers and a few people milling near the check-in area. Her bag rolled to a stop, and she pulled her phone out again, wondering if she'd misunderstood the brief.

A loud engine roared outside, and she glanced up, spotting an enormous pickup truck. Country music blared from inside as the driver's side door swung open and a man stepped out. He was wearing a denim coat with a shearling collar, and as he walked around the front of the truck, his boots sounded on the pavement. Serenity shook her head and returned her attention to her phone. He must be here for someone else.

The automatic doors swung open, and the man walked in, removing his cowboy hat. Their eyes met, and Serenity blinked. Hard. This guy, whoever he was, was seriously one of the hottest men she'd ever seen. He was tall, really tall, and his broad shoulders narrowed into an impossible V at the waist. He gave her a nod before scanning the lobby with a puzzled expression. His crystal blue eyes were sharp as he looked around. His longish blond hair was sporting a serious case of hat head, but that didn't matter. This guy wouldn't have been out of place on Mt. Olympus.

She pulled her eyes away and glanced outside, wondering if maybe she was supposed to meet her driver in the parking lot.

The cowboy slapped his hat on his thigh, drawing her eyes back to him. He glanced at his watch and looked around before finally looking at Serenity. He grinned, his tanned face revealing a set of white teeth.

"Are you by any chance a reporter?" he asked.

"I am," she said, flustered as she caught a whiff of his cologne. "My name's Serenity Adams."

He smelled like what she imagined a forest would smell like if you could capture the scent of snow on pine boughs.

"Austin Rivers. I'm just the man you're looking for," he said, giving her a wink, followed by a cocky grin.

"What? I'm waiting for a driver from The Mended Hearts Ranch. I'm sure they'll be here shortly."

He perched his hat back on his head and grinned at her.

"And that's me."

She glanced between him and the giant pickup idling outside, feeling like her brain just couldn't compute what she was hearing. She looked closer at the side of the pickup and saw the Mended Hearts Ranch logo on the door. This must be her ride, but it definitely wasn't what she'd expected.

"I don't understand."

"I said I'm your driver, Austin. I thought you city girls were quicker on the uptake than this."

Serenity narrowed her eyes. It didn't matter how hot this guy was; his attitude made her grit her teeth. She straightened her spine and swore softly to herself. Even though she was wearing one of her tallest pairs of heels, he towered over her. She opened her mouth and shut it with a snap as he kept talking.

"Anyway, if you're the reporter from *The Globe Trotter*, I'm your driver, and yes, we're going to the Mended Hearts Ranch. If you're coming, let's go. Otherwise, this train leaves the station in about thirty seconds."

He spun on his heel and walked toward the door, not bothering to make sure she was following. Serenity's ears burned, and not-so-nice thoughts rampaged through her head as she grabbed the handle of her bag and followed in his wake. The doors slid open, and once again, the fresh smell of the air hit her nose, forcing her to inhale sharply.

"Smells good out here, doesn't it? Bet it's a darn sight better than that city air you're used to breathing."

She wasn't about to agree with him. If he'd told her water was wet at that moment, she would have argued the point.

"I guess. Where do you want me to put my bag?"

He grabbed the handle, brushing her hand. A little zip worked its way up her arm and back down her spine. Her eyes flew open, startled. He glanced up at her and smiled, crinkling the corners of his eyes so blue it was like the sky had been captured in their depths.

"I'll get it for you," he said, winking again.

He swung the bag into the backseat of the pickup like it was full of feathers before motioning her into the passenger seat. Serenity clambered up into the cab, snagging her heel on the side step before yanking it free and tucking her feet as she smoothed her skirt. What had she gotten herself into?

Chapter Two

Austin

What on earth had Mr. Bohannon gotten him into? When his boss asked him to pick up a reporter from the airport, he'd somehow pictured a rumpled, nerdy guy in a cardigan. Austin walked around the pickup to get in, cursing his boss for omitting to tell him the reporter was, in fact, a woman hotter than the sun. Her long brown hair was so shiny that, for a second, he thought he'd caught his reflection in it.

He glanced over at Serenity as he hopped in and smiled, hoping she'd relax a little. Her light brown eyes reminded him of whiskey and, from the look she was giving him, carried the same sting. He bet that if he stared into them long enough, he'd feel drunk. Austin shook his head and focused on getting out of the airport and not on her long, tanned legs. He'd almost swallowed his tongue when her heel caught on the step, revealing a toned thigh.

"Have you ever been to Wyoming?" he asked.

Dang it, why did he lead with that inane question? Something about this woman turned his mind into a jumble. He knew he'd been a sarcastic jerk in the airport, but somehow, he couldn't control his tongue. She made him feel like a five-year-old kid yanking on a pretty girl's ponytail in hopes she'd notice him.

"No."

He glanced over at her as she looked out the window, drinking in the beauty of the surrounding mountains. He'd better pay attention to the road. She was quiet, and he debated turning up the radio so they wouldn't have to talk, but Mr. Bohannon had been clear about how important it was to make a good impression on this reporter.

"How long are you here for?"

That wasn't much better than his first question, but he hoped she would say more than just six words.

"A week."

Okay. Two words this time. Getting her to talk was about as painful as the time he had a wisdom tooth pulled. She looked tense, and he blamed himself. He'd been so rattled when he spotted her that he knew he probably hadn't made the best impression. Austin glanced over at her again, noting her set expression. Yep, he'd really messed up.

"Where are you from?"

She blew air through her nose, like the ornery mare he'd been trying to break to saddle lately. Wisely, he kept his mouth shut, figuring she wouldn't appreciate the comparison.

"California. And you?"

Hey, maybe they could have a conversation. She'd asked an actual question. He rolled his tight shoulders and tried to relax. Austin felt like he'd touched an electric fence when their hands brushed earlier, and the feeling lingered. Must have been static or something.

"I'm from around here. Lived here my whole life," he said, pausing as he turned onto the highway. "What part of California?"

"L.A. How big is the town where the ranch is?"

"About five hundred. Give or take. The ranch is about five miles from town, though."

She looked at him, turning those big, expressive eyes in his direction. Austin's heart skipped a beat.

"Five hundred people? In the whole town?"

"Well, I didn't mean cattle. That would probably expand the population by a few thousand, though. I suppose you have that many people in a city block where you're from."

"More than that. There's cell service out here, right?" she asked, holding up her phone like it was her last lifeline.

He couldn't help but chuckle. Her forehead was furrowed, and she looked adorable as she glanced around, looking for, he assumed, cell towers.

"We get a little. It's not the best, but you shouldn't be

completely cut off from civilization. This here's a dead patch, though. Once we're closer to town, your phone should work."

She let out a breath and tucked her phone back into her pocket.

"I suppose as long as there's internet at the ranch, I'll be able to work."

"Why do you need internet for that? Aren't you going to interview people? You know, actually talk to them?"

She huffed out a laugh, a soft sound that tugged at something in his chest.

"I have other assignments I'll be working on, too. I need to finish up a story."

"So, you're a travel writer, huh?"

Brilliant question, Austin, he thought. Why was he so muddle-headed around this woman?

"Yep. I travel to resorts and locations and write about what I experience."

He let out a whistle as he imagined a life so different from his daily grind he couldn't quite picture it.

"Must be rough."

She let out that quick laugh again, but this time, it didn't sound happy.

"I know what you're thinking. And you're right. I'm lucky to have my job. Most people would give their right arm for a chance to travel and live the high life. You'd be surprised, though. Never stopping in one place longer than a few weeks can take its toll."

She paused, and the saddest expression crept across her face as she clenched her hands briefly. It was gone like a passing cloud, but he was certain he'd seen it. He waited for her to continue, but she'd gone silent again.

"I bet. Do you have a place in L.A., then? Somewhere to call home?"

She snorted delicately, and a soft blush colored her face.

"I did. I think I still do. I guess... I guess I'm not sure."

That didn't sound good. He glanced at her face again before turning the pickup onto the road that led past the town of Granite. They'd be at the ranch in a few minutes, but he was tempted to go slower, now that he'd gotten her talking. Her voice was soft, lower in pitch than he thought it would be. It reminded him of rich honey being poured out of a jar.

"You're not sure about having a home?"

She shrugged her shoulders and looked out the window again.

"It's complicated. We've been together for a long time. I'm sure everything will be fine."

Dang it, he thought to himself, cursing in his head. He should've known a woman this beautiful wouldn't be single. Heck, she was only going to be here for a week, and from the sounds of it, she'd be jetting off to somewhere exotic when she left. Why had the thought even entered his mind? Must be the altitude or something. He needed to change the subject.

"You should have cell service now."

She whipped her phone out faster than a gunfighter and peered at the screen, a hopeful expression on her sweet face. Out of the corner of his eye, Austin watched it crumple as she paged down her screen and hit the button to lock her phone. Briefly, he thought he'd like to punch whoever made her look like that. The town appeared as they rounded the bend. He wondered what she thought of it and glanced back at her. She was looking out the window again but didn't seem to focus on anything particular.

"Need anything before we head to the ranch?"

"What? Oh, no. Thank you. I'm fine."

He nodded and kept cruising, searching for a safe conversation topic. Austin didn't really know what to say, but he knew he wanted to keep her talking.

"I hope you brought some winter clothes. It's spring, but it gets pretty chilly here at night."

Geez, this woman had turned him into a real conversational master. He closed one eye and hoped she didn't think he was as lame as he felt. It didn't help that he knew she was taken. The soft scent of her perfume drifted his way, distracting him further. She smelled like an orchard full of blossoms, delicate and sweet.

"I'll be fine. Are we getting close?"

"Yeah, we'll be at the ranch house in about five minutes."

She nodded and went back to looking out the window. He turned up the music and nodded his head along to the beat as he drove. She glanced over at him, and he spotted the corners of her mouth turned up slightly before they fell back into place. What he wouldn't give to see a full smile from those gorgeous lips.

He really needed to get a grip. Here he was, mooning over this beautiful woman like a calf. Austin tapped his fingers on the steering wheel as they drove under the arch that led the way to the place he called both work and home. He'd been lucky when Mr. Bohannon had offered him a job. He'd been working on his brother's ranch a few miles away, but they'd chafed against each other.

His brother was the oldest and had inherited the place when their dad passed a few years ago. They had different ideas on how to run a ranch, and eventually, Austin gave up trying to make him see it his way. When the old Rainey place sold, the town speculated for a solid month about the new owner. Would there be any jobs? That was one thing that truly mattered in a small town. All gossip aside, people needed a place to work if they were going to make it in the Wyoming wilderness.

No one knew Jim Bohannon, but when he offered Austin a job, he didn't care about his new boss's past. All he cared about was getting out from under his brother's thumb and starting fresh. Did it rankle getting busted down to a regular ranch hand when he'd enjoyed almost free rein at his brother's place? A little. But so far, his boss had proved fair. His job was to care for the stock that would be used for trail rides, and that made up for it. Eventually, he'd lead the trail rides and wrangle the guests. He loved horses and found working with them peaceful. No, he wouldn't trade his new position for anything. It was the first time he'd felt like he'd been home and part of an actual family.

Austin snorted, lost in thought. The guys he worked with were a strange bunch, but somehow, they all fit together. They were still learning the ropes and figuring out their own pecking order, but it was a solid group of guys. He pulled into the ranch yard and watched Serenity's face as she took in the main house. It was an impressive structure, and on a blue sky day like today, it looked even better. He put the truck in park and hustled to help her with her bag as he wondered what this city girl would think of a place like this.

As she stepped down from the cab, she stumbled a little on her heels, falling against his broad chest. His arms wrapped around her automatically, and for a second, he imagined what it would be like if she came to him willingly. Her hair smelled amazing, and she felt so tiny in his arms. She stepped back and squared her shoulders.

"Might want to trade those fancy heels in for something a little sturdier," he said with a smile, hoping she wouldn't take offense.

"I'll be fine. I can run in them, and I'm sure I can get around here just fine in them, too."

He lost his train of thought as he stared at her mouth, which was currently quirked in irritation. Her eyes narrowed, and he snapped to attention.

"Let me take you inside to meet Mr. Bohannon."

"I can take myself," she said, spinning on her heels.

He cleared his throat, amused by her reaction.

"Do you want your bag?"

She stopped and turned, her fair skin going markedly pink. He dragged her bag out of the back seat and placed it on the ground, wondering briefly what on earth she'd crammed into that thing. Bricks? She stalked over and took the handle.

"Thanks."

Austin watched her walk to the ranch house, steady and sure of herself as she dragged her bag behind her. He shook his head as he hopped back into his truck and headed for the barn.

Chapter Three

Serenity

She marched up the walk towards the imposing house, refusing to look back over her shoulder at that infuriating man. She was breathing hard, and little pulses of energy were shooting through her skin. The wheels of her bag caught on a piece of gravel, skewing to the side and almost pulling her with it.

Serenity risked a glance and saw the back of Austin's pickup as he drove off. Hopefully, he hadn't seen that. She took a deep breath and turned back to the house before coming to a stop at the door. Should she knock? Just go in? As she raised her hand, the door suddenly swung open, startling her.

A tall man with vibrant green eyes stared at her like she had two heads, blinking slowly. A slow smile spread across his face, and she felt her own face flush at his appraisal. His black hair curled softly over his collar.

"Well, hello there. Where did you come from?"

"The airport," Serenity said. "Who are you?"

He stepped outside, joining her on the spacious deck, and nodded once before placing his cowboy hat on his head.

"Name's Colt. You must be the reporter?"

"Yes, I'm Serenity Adams. Is Mr. Bohannon around?"

"He is. Martha will help you get settled. I'd help you myself, but I've got to get to the south pasture. Nice meeting you, miss."

He grabbed her hand and held it before placing a kiss on it and walking down the steps.

Serenity stood there with her mouth open as she watched him. Did gorgeous cowboys grow on trees out here or something? She shook her head and turned back towards the door, starting when she saw a small woman standing there with a wry grin on her face. Her pure white hair was pulled back into a severe bun, but her face was pleasant.

"Distracting, isn't he?" the woman asked.

Serenity laughed and nodded, feeling the tension she'd stored between her shoulder blades melt away.

"You could say that. Are you Martha?"

"Where are my manners? Of course, child, I'm Martha. You are Serenity, I take it? Mr. Bohannon told me you were coming. Come on in, and let's get you settled."

The small woman beckoned and cocked her head to

the side, looking for all the world like a small, interested bird. Her dark eyes sparkled as Serenity struggled not to chuckle at the picture she made. Ever since she'd gotten there, she'd felt almost like an animal at a zoo exhibit. Over here, we have the rare California girl, not usually seen in the Wyoming territory. Serenity snorted, surprising herself.

"Sorry," she said, blushing. "It's nice to meet you, Martha. I think I'm supposed to stay here at the ranch, according to the briefing I have."

"Of course, of course. Let's get you to your room so you can relax for a bit."

The tiny woman grabbed Serenity's bag and hefted it up the stairs like it weighed nothing.

"I can get that," Serenity said as she hustled after the woman.

Martha made it to the top of the stairs and waved her free hand.

"Right this way."

Serenity paused at the top of the stairs, admiring the way the wooden beams shone as they slanted overhead. The light-colored wood made the place feel even bigger than it was. She glanced over the railing, looking down on the open area below. Several couches were arranged in front of one of the biggest fireplaces she'd ever seen. She glanced down the hall and realized she'd lost Martha.

"Martha?"

She hustled down the hall and came to a stop as Martha's head poked out from a doorway.

"In here, dear. We've put you in the Canyon Suite."

Serenity walked into the room and paused, amazed by the attention to detail. The suite was enormous and dominated by a giant antique four-poster bed. The muted earth tones of the paint and drapes soothed her soul. She walked over to the windows and parted the drapes, gasping as the mountains in the distance came into view.

"It's so beautiful," she said, half to herself.

"It is at that, isn't it? A view like that never gets old."

Serenity turned as Martha bustled around the room, straightening pictures and running a rag over the dresser.

"Thank you so much for showing me to my room. Is Mr. Bohannon available? I've got a few questions for him before I write my article."

Martha's face stilled for a second and Serenity leaned in, sensing something was wrong. The older woman seemed to catch herself and smiled, turning back to her tasks.

"He's busy right now, lass, but I'll make sure you get to speak to him before supper. We serve that right at six, ranch style. That will give you enough time to get settled in, rest a little, and join us."

"I usually only have a light meal," Serenity said before Martha jumped in.

"It's mandatory for all guests to attend. If you're here, you are family, and we all eat together. Well, at least we sure try," Martha said, her tone showing she didn't want an argument. "I'll see you then."

The little woman bustled out and shut the door

before Serenity could reply. What on earth did she mean by that? Everyone ate together? Serenity had a flash of Austin's wicked smile and felt her cheeks flush. Hopefully, the woman meant guests only.

Serenity sat on the bed, sinking down into the plush depths, and stared at her suitcase. This had to be one of the oddest assignments she'd ever been on. As she looked at the room, she shrugged and let out a short laugh. At least the place was clean, spacious, and, to be honest, decadently gorgeous. She fished her phone out of her bag, looked at the screen, and bit her lip.

Nothing from Chad. Still. She leaned back on the pillows and went through her texts first before answering the multitude of emails crowding her inbox. She sent a quick email to Herman, letting him know she'd arrived, before setting her phone down and closing her eyes.

Should she text Chad? Again? She picked up her phone and stared at the black screen, trying to figure out what to do. She put it down on the bed cover, face down, and focused instead on unpacking. Her legs felt like lead as she stood, and a wave of tiredness threatened to buckle her legs.

Serenity slipped off her heels and grabbed the soft carpet underfoot with her toes. Now that felt good. She sorted through her bag and tried to figure out what would be appropriate for supper at a ranch house. She'd focused on bringing casual clothes since she figured she'd be outside a good portion of the time. She tapped her finger on her lips as she went through her shirts, finally picking one that she thought would work.

Now, what else to wear? She glanced at the one pair of sneakers she'd brought and shook her head. She felt almost naked without her heels, no matter what the infuriating cowboy said. That settled it, she thought, pulling out her black skinny jeans that looked amazing with heels. That problem solved, she finished unpacking and went into the adjoining bathroom to change.

The marble counter gleamed as she flipped on the light and her eyes widened. This was certainly a nice place, considering it was in the middle of nowhere. She wasn't sure exactly who Jim Bohannon was, but he obviously was well experienced with the finer things in life. She ran her hand over the counter before plopping her makeup bag on it and getting changed. Once she was dressed, she glanced in the mirror and shrugged, mostly happy with her appearance. She hoped the dressy top wasn't too much for a ranch dinner and laughed. It wasn't like she'd ever been to a ranch dinner before.

Serenity looked at her watch and chewed on her lip. Still two hours until she needed to be downstairs. She went back to her bag, pulled out her laptop, and flipped it open. While she waited, she'd see what she could find out about the elusive owner of the ranch. Her first search, done hurriedly the night she packed for the trip, had pulled up almost no information.

She typed in his name into her search engine and filtered through the results, finding only a few that were pertinent. Unfortunately, they were local pieces that simply mentioned the sale of the ranch. Intrigued, she searched for the name of the ranch, figuring there had to be a record of the owner, but once again, she found nothing. Something about this just wasn't right. Anyone who could afford to buy a ranch of this size had to be, if not well off, at least known.

A knock at the door startled her, and she quickly closed her laptop and slipped it in the bag before hurrying over to the door. As she opened it, Martha came into view.

"Mr. Bohannon will see you now," she said, motioning for her to follow.

Serenity hustled to keep up with the tiny house-keeper as she walked down the hall at a fast clip. Suddenly, she came to a screeching halt and pointed at a door at the end of the hall.

"He's in there. Once you're done with your talk, come on down for dinner. Most everyone should filter in by then."

"Yes, ma'am," she said. "Thank you."

Martha nodded and hurried back down the hall. Serenity took a deep sniff and smiled. Whatever they were going to serve tonight, it sure smelled good. She turned, rapped on the door, and waited for Mr. Bohannon to answer. This was going to be interesting.

"Enter."

She took a deep breath and walked in, fully armed with a smile. The lighting in the room was dim, and it took a second for her eyes to adjust. She spotted a man seated at a desk by the window.

"Please, take a seat," he said.

"Mr. Bohannon, I'm Serenity Adams. Herman asked me to take this story. I gather you two know each other?" Serenity asked as she sank down into the leather chair.

She could see the man's shoulders shake slightly with what she thought was laughter.

"You could say that. We met twenty or so years ago. Is everything shipshape with your room? If you need anything, just ask Martha, and she'll make sure you're taken care of."

"Oh, it's fine. You have a gorgeous place, Mr. Bohannon."

"Please call me Jim."

"Jim, I have a few preliminary questions for you as I get ready to write this piece. I like to have a feel for the owner's vision of the property. Would you mind answering a few questions?"

"Actually, tonight isn't a good time for me. Maybe we can talk in a couple of days. That will give you a chance to meet everyone and see the place. Develop your own impressions."

Serenity reared her head back, shocked. Typically, when she interviewed the owner of a resort, they were all too happy to talk about themselves and their property.

"I see. Well, thank you for inviting me here. I hope we can talk soon," she said, standing. "Will you be joining us for dinner? Martha mentioned everyone here eats family style."

"No."

He swiveled his chair, effectively cutting off any further questions. Serenity stared at the back of his head for a second before turning on her heels and walking to the door. She paused, one hand on the knob, and looked over her shoulder before shaking her head.

She left and pushed the door shut, questions whizzing around her brain like angry wasps. As she walked down the hall towards the stairs, she couldn't help but wonder what everyone else was going to be like.

Chapter Four

Austin

Austin walked into the dining room and raised his eyebrows as he saw the spread Martha had laid out on the table. She was going all out tonight. For a second, he thought he'd gotten the month wrong and that it was Thanksgiving. He sniffed appreciatively, his stomach rumbling as he stood next to his buddy, Colt.

"Hey man, how's that new mare you're breaking?" Colt asked as he reached for a glistening dinner roll, only to have his hand smacked by Martha.

"We're waiting for Serenity, you heathen," she said, shaking her head. "She should be here any minute."

Austin's pulse spiked, and he struggled to focus on what Colt had asked.

"Everything's fine," he said, glancing up the stairs.

Colt grinned, giving his friend a knowing look. He leaned closer to Austin so no one would overhear.

"Five-to-one odds you didn't hear a thing I just asked you."

Austin snapped his head around and glared at his friend.

"Whatever, I heard you. And I answered you."

Colt snorted and shook his head.

"I'll let it go, but I know what's distracting you. My guess is she's got pretty brown hair, eyes like a doe, and legs that..."

Austin's eyes narrowed and his jaw tensed as he gritted his teeth. He pried them apart to answer, but Colt beat him to it, an interesting look passing across his face.

"So it's like that, huh?"

Austin shouldered past his friend, needing to breathe for a second. Why on earth was he acting like this? Like he had some sort of claim on the woman he'd literally met just a few hours ago? He gave Doc, the staff veterinarian, a brief nod as he walked past. He clapped Jack on the arm, but his friend seemed preoccupied.

He felt his eyes drawn to the top of the stairs, and his breath caught in his throat as he watched Serenity walk down. Her slim jeans hugged every curve of her long legs. She paused at the foot of the stairs, and he walked towards her without even thinking about it. He grabbed a glass of wine off the table on his way.

"There you are. I thought we'd have to send out a search party," he said, handing her the glass.

She sipped it, her eyes widening.

"That is amazing wine."

"Mr. Bohannon doesn't skimp on the house wine, that's for sure. What do you think of the place so far?"

He half-wanted to put his elbow out so she'd take his arm, but paused, seeing the laughing eyes of Colt, Doc, and Jack as they watched him.

"It's a nice place, that's for sure. The rooms are very well done," she said, pausing and giving him a thoughtful look. "I have a question about your boss, though."

Martha bustled into the room, carrying a platter loaded with a gigantic turkey, interrupting Serenity. Austin heard her stomach growl, and he smiled. He remembered the first time he'd had some of Martha's cooking. If he kept eating up here at the ranch house, he was going to need to exercise a lot more. He pulled a chair out for Serenity and swept his arm out in a half-joking gesture.

Serenity's perfectly shaped eyebrow rose, and she almost smiled before picking her seat. He grabbed the chair next to her and cursed softly as Doc claimed the one on her other side. He wanted her all to himself, a feeling he didn't quite understand. He picked up a glass of wine and drained half of it in a gulp as he tried not to listen to Doc's charming voice.

"I don't believe I've had the pleasure," Doc said, leaning toward Serenity. "I'm Doc Watts."

"Serenity Adams. I thought for a second you were going to say Dr. Watson," Serenity said. "What do you do here?"

Doc snorted a laugh and nodded his head toward the other cowboys who were lining up at the table.

"More like Doc Holliday, I hope. I'm the vet, but occasionally, I stitch up the cowboys when they get a little reckless."

"Is that something they do often?" Serenity asked, tipping her head to the side.

Austin looked at the shiny hair that fell over her shoulder and downed the rest of his glass. It was going to be a long evening if this kept up. She'd been all but taciturn on the trip here, and now she'd turned into a chatterbox with Doc.

"More often than you'd think," Doc said, leaning forward so he could wink at Austin. "Rivers here in particular has been in more scrapes than most in the short time I've been here."

"I work with horses," Austin said, feeling a flush work its way up his chest to his neck. "Sometimes they get a little rowdy."

"And so do you," Doc said, winking at Serenity.

She glanced at Austin, and his blood pressure surged as her soft brown eyes met his. He glanced around for more wine and settled for water instead. That was smarter, anyway.

"You work with horses?" Serenity asked as she pivoted to give him her full attention.

"Yes, ma'am. I'm the lead wrangler at the ranch."

"Wrangler? What does that mean?"

"I train the horses, break them to ride, and eventually, once we have guests, I'll take them out on trail rides. Do you like horses?"

"I never liked that term, breaking," Serenity said, placing her napkin in her lap and picking at it a little. "But yes, I love horses."

Austin grinned so widely he thought his teeth might fall out.

"I never thought a city girl would be interested in horses. You'll have to come by the corrals tomorrow and meet a few of them. I have a nice little mare I'd love for you to meet."

"Don't get him started on horses," Doc said, reclaiming her attention. "He'll never stop yakking."

"And don't ask him about rare diseases. He'll talk your ears off. He likes to do that while we eat," Austin said with a shudder.

His voice hardened, and Doc glanced over the top of Serenity's head, meeting Austin's gaze with a surprised look.

"That's enough talking, boys," Martha said, settling into a chair across from Serenity. "It's time to eat. You look like a stiff wind could carry you off, Serenity. Dig in."

Dishes were passed around, and silence reigned for a few minutes as everyone filled their plates. A loud bang echoed from the entryway, and everyone paused. Austin glanced up and grinned at Hawk as he walked in. The young cowboy was flushed and looked like he'd been in a footrace.

"Sorry, Miss Martha," Hawk mumbled as he grabbed a chair. "I lost track of time."

The little woman smiled and passed him a plate.

"I'll let it slide this time."

Everyone chuckled, and Hawk blushed. Austin leaned closer to Serenity, inhaling that sweet scent of apple blossoms as he spoke into her ear.

"That's Hawk. He's the youngest of the bunch."

"He seems sweet," Serenity said.

"He's a good kid. Been through a lot."

"I bet you all have some interesting stories," she said as she passed the dish of potatoes to Doc.

"We do. Some more than others, but we're a unique bunch, I guess you could say. Not a fan of potatoes?"

Serenity shook her head slightly.

"I'm not that hungry."

Austin looked back at her, remembering how loudly her stomach had growled when Martha brought in the main course.

"Could've fooled me," he said.

She shot him a look and turned deliberately toward Doc, cutting Austin out of the conversation. He played with the green beans on his plate as he berated himself. Why couldn't he say the right things in front of her? He'd never had this problem before. He reached for the bottle of wine in the center of the table and refilled his glass.

He'd never been one for wine, preferring beer, but Martha was a stickler. She insisted beer had no place at the dining table, and after a few weeks, he'd agreed with her. He sipped slowly, determined not to overindulge and make an even bigger fool of himself. He tried not to listen to Doc's lively chatter and turned toward Jack, bumping his friend with his elbow.

"Why so distracted, Jack?"

Jack's dark eyebrows furrowed as he glanced at Austin.

"Got a lot on my mind. How's Tilly doing?"

Tilly was the little mare he thought Serenity would like. She'd had a hock injury a few weeks ago and was finally healed up to where she could be ridden. He momentarily lost the thread of the conversation as he imagined a romantic ride with Serenity by his side before remembering to answer Jack.

"She's better. I don't know when I've met a nicer mare."

Jack nodded and swept his fork through the mashed potatoes on his plate.

"That's good. Want to go to the bar later?"

Austin looked at his friend and kept from grinning. Barely. He had an idea that Jack wanted to go to the bar to do more than drink. The beautiful bartender, Cassie, probably had something to do with that.

"Sorry, man. Not tonight. I need to be up early."

"Fine."

Jack lapsed back into silence, continuing to stir his potatoes absentmindedly.

"You gonna eat those or play with them?"

"What? Oh, sorry," Jack said.

Austin snuck a glance at Serenity, feeling his hand tighten as he heard her musical laugh. He wanted to be the one to coax that beautiful sound out of her, not Doc. He focused on his meal, cleaning his plate.

"Austin?"

He shook his head, startled, and met Serenity's concerned eyes.

"I'm sorry. What did you say?"

Serenity smiled briefly, a dimple he'd never noticed winking in and out of sight.

"I asked if you knew anything about your boss. I like to get a background on the resort owners when I write my pieces."

"Oh. Yeah, I guess I know a little. What do you want to know?"

She folded her napkin in her lap, fiddling with the hem before she spoke.

"I just can't find much about him online, and he didn't want to answer my questions earlier. It just felt a little odd."

Austin nodded thoughtfully before shrugging.

"I see. Well, I haven't known him for long, I guess, but he seems like a good guy."

She let out a brief laugh, warming his heart, even though he wasn't sure why.

"That's exactly what Doc said when I asked him."

"Miss, they say you're a travel writer," Hawk said, interrupting Austin's response. "What do you write about?"

Serenity smiled at the young cowboy and put down her fork.

"Many things. I mostly cover resorts, like this place."

"Have you been to some cool places?" Hawk asked, his voice eager. "I've never left the state, see, and I'm curious."

Serenity smiled, a genuine one that took Austin's breath away. He decided that somehow, some way, he was going to make her smile like that for him. He listened as she described one of her most recent adventures. The table quieted, enthralled with her tale. Even Jack stopped sulking and listened.

Once she was done, Hawk's eyes lit like candles. Much like the bird of prey he was named after, they were an odd yellowish-brown color. Austin smiled, happy to see the young man so interested in something. Typically, he was so shy you couldn't get two words out of the kid.

"Wow, ma'am. Someday I'd like to see that for myself."

The rest of the group laughed, and Hawk flushed, looking uncomfortable. Austin's heart went out to him.

"That sounds like a good plan," Austin said, folding his napkin and putting it next to his plate. "You can never be too well-traveled."

Hawk's throat bobbed a little as he swallowed hard and shot Austin a grateful smile.

"Well said."

Serenity's quiet voice made his heart leap. He wanted to bask in her approval, but Martha stood up and began clearing the dishes. Serenity jumped up to help, startling Austin. He'd expected her to act like a guest and expect to be catered to.

"Miss, you don't need to do that," Martha said, flustered.

"Yes, I do. That was a wonderful meal. You can't be expected to do these dishes yourself."

Austin's face heated as he realized that every night, that was exactly what happened. The cowboys ate their fill and headed outside to talk and drink. He stood, nearly knocking over his chair in his haste.

"I'll help, too."

Doc's laugh cracked like a whip through the dining room, but he stilled when Austin glared at him.

"Sorry. That's a great idea, Serenity. We'll all help."

Austin bit back a retort and focused instead on stacking as many plates as he could hold. Martha looked befuddled as Hawk grabbed the stack of dishes she was carrying and headed into the kitchen.

Within a few minutes, everyone had their sleeves rolled up, and Jack was arguing good-naturedly with Doc over who was going to dry what. Austin claimed the spot next to Serenity at the sink and handed her dishes as she carefully hand-washed each one.

He caught Martha's approving glance and smiled at her before returning to his task.

"Did you want to come see the mare tomorrow?" he asked, feeling strangely shy.

Serenity rinsed the plate she was holding before answering him.

"I never pass up an opportunity to meet a horse. I've got a few things to do, but after that, I'll be happy to meet you at the corrals."

He felt a bubble of delight swell in his chest at her words and nodded, not trusting his voice just then. He handed her the last plate and looked around the crowded room.

"Thank you," he said, speaking quietly so no one would overhear.

Serenity looked startled as she rinsed the dish and passed it to Doc.

"For what?"

He glanced around the room and back at her.

"For reminding us we're all a family and we should help each other out. We'd forgotten that."

"Oh. No big deal," she said, shrugging and giving him another smile that showed the dimple in her left cheek.

An urge to kiss that cute dimple overtook Austin, and he turned away, wiping his hands on his jeans.

"Did you want to sit outside and look at the stars?" he asked, handing her a towel.

She wiped her hands and was about to answer when a loud ding issued from her back pocket. Serenity handed him the towel and looked at her phone. Her face creased into a frown, and he put a hand on her arm.

"Is everything okay?"

"What? Oh, yes. It's fine. I'm going to go up to my room."

She wandered away, staring at her screen. As she got to the door, she tucked her phone back into her pocket and scanned the room, finally spotting Martha, who was putting the plates away.

"Thank you for the meal, Martha. It was one of the best I've had."

Austin watched the tiny woman's face brighten like the sun at the compliment, and his heart flipped in his chest. Serenity might be a city girl, but she had manners that put all of them to shame. He watched her walk out of the kitchen and wished he could follow.

Chapter Five

Serenity

She flopped like a fish, trying to get comfortable in the enormous bed. Serenity sighed and stared at the ceiling, watching as sunlight peeped in through the curtains. It wasn't the bed's fault she hadn't slept, she thought, as she flipped over yet again and punched her pillow. Briefly, she wished that pillow's name was Chad.

She'd enjoyed herself the night before, talking with the cowboys, before getting a text from her boyfriend. After trying to call him, only to go to voicemail, she'd sent a few texts before giving up for the night and turning off her phone. She squinched her eyes shut, not wanting to think about Chad for one more second, and the image of Austin's handsome face floated in front of her. Groaning, she gave up the idea of sleeping and sat up, scooched against the soft pillows, and automatically reached for her phone.

Once it loaded, it went off like a Roman candle, chiming as a bunch of texts, missed calls, and emails came through. Serenity's eyebrow quirked as she saw a text from her best friend Lily. They'd been friends since college and roommates until Serenity met Chad. With the way things were going, they might very well be roommates again.

Hey girlie, how's the wild west? Meet any handsome cowboys?

She laughed and typed a reply.

It's wild for sure. What would they say out here? You can't swing a cat without hitting a good-looking man. You should come and see for yourself.

Lily responded, making Serenity snort with laughter.

Don't hog them all to yourself! Second thought, go hog wild! Wish I could be there (and not just for the men with spurs.) Miss you!

She thought about texting Lily with the latest from Chad, but decided against it, opting instead for a laughing emoji. She scanned through the rest of her texts, not seeing anything important. Chad hadn't even bothered to reply after dropping the equivalent of a cryptic bomb by text and then ignoring her for the rest of the evening. What did he even mean when he'd said he hoped the job would keep her away for a while? She heaved an irritated sigh and flipped over to her voice-mail to listen to her messages.

Her editor, Herm, had left a voicemail asking for her first impressions. The next voicemail was an urgent message about her car's extended warranty, which made her laugh. She didn't even own a car. She deleted the message and went to her email app to type up a quick reply to Herm as she glanced at her watch. It was seven o'clock here, which meant it was already nine back home.

All of her morning tasks completed, she put her phone face down on the nightstand and spread her hands across the exquisite comforter. Doc had invited her to stop by his ranch clinic to see how the ranch took care of its many animals, and Austin wanted her to stop by the corrals. So far, she'd been frustrated in her attempts to get more information about Jim Bohannon. What was his story?

He'd told her he'd talk to her after she saw more of the ranch. Anything was preferable to sitting around thinking about Chad. She got up and headed into the bathroom to wash away the nasty feeling under her skin. Did he really want to break up with her over a simple job? She hopped in the shower, turning up the heat full blast, and stood under the water for a few minutes.

Chad had always supported her career in the past. Heck, he'd even gone with her a few times when he had time off from his job as a financial consultant. Lately, though, he'd been distant, and if she was being honest with herself, absent more times than not. She shook her head and started washing her hair, snorting as the song from *South Pacific* came to mind. Maybe that's just what she needed to do.

Feeling immeasurably better, she stepped out of the shower and dried herself off with a plush towel. This may be the Wild West, but Mr. Bohannon sure had pulled out all the stops for his guest's comfort. She got dressed, picking out a clean pair of jeans and a long-sleeved tee. She glanced at her shoe selection and shook her head. She hadn't thought about footwear when she'd packed for this trip. Typically, she ended up wearing a combination of heels, wedges, and sandals on her assignments, but this place was different. She grabbed a pair of high-heeled boots and slipped them on.

She blow-dried her hair and thought about her options for the morning. Doc had invited her to see his clinic, and she was intrigued by the good-looking veterinarian. She didn't know what went into running a ranch, and it would be interesting to see the different animals. What were guests supposed to do here? After tying up her hair in a ponytail, she put on some mascara and lip gloss before nodding to herself in the mirror. No time like the present.

Serenity grabbed her bag, making sure she had a fresh notebook, pen, and her phone. Even though everything was digital these days, she still liked to take notes the old-fashioned way. She walked down the stairs, sniffing as a decadent smell wafted into her nostrils. It was heavy with cinnamon and something she couldn't quite place.

The dining table was laden with pastries, and her stomach gurgled as she looked longingly at a giant cinnamon roll that had to be bigger than her head.

"Good morning," Martha said, her voice cheerful.

"Good morning. I was just going to thank you for

that wonderful meal last night, but it looks like you outdid yourself with breakfast."

"This? Oh, it's just a few things to tide everyone over until lunch. The boys have already headed out to work, but it looks like they left plenty."

"Are there any other guests staying here?" Serenity asked, looking back up at the landing.

The place had been quiet, and she had seen no one else at dinner the night before.

"Not yet, but we're expecting a few people to check in later today. Maybe you can interview a few of them for your article. But for now, it looks like you've got your pick."

Serenity eyed the cinnamon rolls again. She wasn't one for breakfast, but a place like this could change your mind. Martha watched her keenly and bustled over.

"Here, they taste even better than they look, or so I've been told," she said, handing Serenity a roll on a plate. "I don't want to brag."

"I don't know. I shouldn't," Serenity said, breaking off a piece to take a small bite.

A multitude of flavors washed over her tongue, and she closed her eyes in pure bliss as she chewed.

"What on earth is in this recipe?" she asked, looking at Martha in wonder.

"A little of this and that. It's an old family secret. Take anything else you want. Whatever's left over will go to town later, so it won't go to waste. Just holler if you need anything. There are a few pamphlets of activities and a map of the place over there by the door."

The little woman disappeared into the kitchen.

Serenity kept chewing, nodding in delight. One thing was for certain: anyone coming here to heal their hearts could drown their sorrows in the amazing food. She licked the last of the icing off her fingers and walked to the door, stopping by the table to look at the brochures.

A few were for the local town and mentioned shopping, bike riding, and other touristy things to do. She made a mental note to see if she could borrow a car later to explore the town. On the wall was a list of ranch activities, including horseback riding, hiking, and nature walks. A full-color map laid out each building and its purpose, as well as the sites of future attractions. Serenity pulled out her phone and took a picture of the map before grabbing a few of the brochures. She walked out onto the steps and paused, taking in the open spaces and hills that surrounded her.

The morning sun painted the surrounding mountains with a soft glow, taking her breath away again. What would it be like living in a place where you had a million-dollar view sitting right outside your door? She'd seen some amazing places, but this ranch called to her soul in a way no other place had. Feeling fanciful, she stepped off the porch and wandered down the walk. Where to go first?

Her thoughts were interrupted by a high-pitched squeal, and she looked around to see where it had come from. A set of corrals with a state-of-the-art horse barn seemed the most logical choice. Serenity picked her way across the gravel on her way to the barn, thinking about Austin. He'd said he broke horses, which called up an image in her mind of cruel bits and harsh actions.

When she'd been little, her mother had taken her to a nearby stable for riding lessons. She'd seen a few of the trainers working with horses, and it had turned her stomach, searing the image of a beautiful horse, terrified of its trainer, into her mind. She walked faster as an even louder squeal broke the silence.

She was almost jogging by the time she reached the corral and came to a halt right by the gate. A horse stood by, breathing hard in the crisp morning air. Its painted black and white sides were heaving as it raised its head up and down. Austin was standing on the horse's side, talking quietly and stroking its muscular neck. The horse squealed again, stamping a hoof hard on the ground.

Serenity saw the horse's mouth and leaned her head to the side. This was something new. Instead of a bridle, complete with a spade bit that could bite into the soft tissues of the horse's mouth, it was wearing a halter with a simple rope. Austin continued speaking quietly, almost singing to the horse. She leaned forward to catch what he was saying.

"There's a good girl, it's okay. There's no need to fight. I won't hurt you."

The horse stamped again and tossed its head before lowering it to the ground. Serenity watched as Austin gently placed a blanket across its withers. The skin on the massive back twitched slightly as he eased it into place, all the while whispering. She caught her breath as the horse stamped again before settling and blowing out a little huff of acceptance.

"Bravo!" she said, unable to keep quiet.

The horse whipped its head around, and Serenity glimpsed Austin's incredibly blue eyes looking startled, just as the horse shied to the left, right into him. She heard Austin grunt as he was shoved into the fence, knocking his head hard on the top rail. The horse let out an angry squeal before taking off, ripping its halter rope out of Austin's hand. The cowboy slumped against the fence, barely missing the flying hooves.

Serenity didn't even think twice as she darted between the rails of the gate and across the corral, swearing softly to herself for wearing heels. They sank into the soft surface, making the few yards feel like a mile. Austin still hadn't moved. She made it to his side and knelt, pushing his cowboy hat back and shifting his head into her lap.

"Austin, are you okay?"

She carefully felt around his scalp for any wounds. He didn't answer right away, and her heart rate picked up. He didn't look injured, and she couldn't feel any blood, but he'd taken a hard rap to the head. She called his name again, feeling panicked. Should she call 9-1-1? Was that something you even did out here in the wilderness?

Austin groaned and adjusted his head, opening his blue eyes and looking right into hers.

"Am I in heaven?" he asked.

His smile nearly stopped her heart. She let out the breath she didn't even realize she was holding and surprised them both by bursting into tears.

Chapter Six

Austin

His head reeled, and not just from the rap he'd taken off the fence. Lying here, with his head in Serenity's soft lap, was as close to Heaven as he thought he'd ever get while he was still breathing. Her beautiful brown eyes teared up suddenly, and he flipped over, reluctantly surrendering his position, and reached up to touch her face as he knelt next to her.

"Hey, I'm okay. You don't need to cry," he said, gently thumbing away her tears.

Her shoulders heaved as she sobbed, trying to hide her face. He wrapped his arms around her and held tight.

"I don't know why I'm crying. I'm sorry."

"Hey, I didn't know you cared that much," he said, leaning back on his heels and tilting her face up.

She snorted and backhanded the tears from her cheeks.

"It's not that. I mean, it's not like I want you to get hurt, but I never cry. Ever. I can't even think of the last time I actually cried."

"Sounds to me like you needed to let some emotion out. Wanna talk about it?"

He craned his neck to the side and tried to get her to look at him. She reluctantly met his eyes, and the pain he saw reflected in her gaze made his heart clench.

"No," she said, stumbling as she tried to get up. "I'm fine. I'm sorry I interrupted your training session."

"You don't look fine to me," Austin said under his breath, holding her arm to help her stand.

She gave him a look, and he stuck his tongue out at her, hoping to get her to laugh. The dimple on her cheek winked briefly before she finally gave up and smiled. His heart eased a little as he joined her and started brushing the corral dirt off his jeans. He glanced over at her and saw she was doing the same, struggling to balance on her heeled boots.

He raised an eyebrow, and she flapped a hand at him.

"I know, I know. I should have brought better shoes."

"I'm not judging. You do you."

That won him another smile, and she laughed almost to herself as she finished brushing the dirt off her backside.

"I typically do. Are you sure you're okay? It looked

like you got knocked out. We should probably get you to a doctor. Let me see your head."

She reached up and gently parted his hair, searching his scalp. The feel of her fingers in his hair was almost too much to take. He stepped back, desperately needing a little distance before he did something he might regret.

"I've had worse. I'm fine. It just knocked the wind out of me, that's all. Hey, while you're here, wanna meet the horses? I need to grab Sally over there and show her to her stall."

She cocked her head to the side as she looked him over. He stuck his tongue out again, and she rolled her eyes.

"Fine. Men. I swear."

She brushed off her jeans and looked over at the mare, who was eying them warily from the other side of the corral. Austin glanced at Serenity before walking over to the mare. He held out his hand, and she reluctantly came to him.

"There's a good girl. We'll come back to this tomorrow, okay? You were doing well there."

Sally blew a shuddering breath and nosed his hand, lowering her head. He wrapped an arm around her neck and leaned into her before grabbing the rope and leading her towards the barn. Serenity watched, edging back out of the way to make sure the mare had plenty of space. He nodded at her and led the mare down the alley into her stall.

Once he got Sally turned around, he eased the halter off and scratched the mare behind her ears. She was a nervous creature, and today was the first day he'd ever gotten a blanket on her. He wished he'd been able to get a little further and earn more of her trust, but tomorrow was another day. Hopefully, today's minor episode wouldn't be repeated. He didn't blame Serenity; she had no way of knowing how skittish Sally was. He gave her another scratch before closing the stall door.

"Here, I hope this is alright," Serenity said, walking towards him with a flake of hay in a net and a bucket of water. "Again, I'm sorry I messed up your training session."

Austin's eyebrows flew up to his hairline. He hadn't expected this city girl to know what he'd need next.

"Thanks," he said, hefting the bucket over the stall door and placing it on the hook. "How'd you know? Have you had horses before?"

Austin almost missed the look of longing that flashed across Serenity's face as he hung the hay net in the front corner of the stall.

"There was a riding stable outside the town where I'm from. My mom took me to riding lessons there, but she couldn't afford to board a horse, not after my father left. I always dreamed that someday I'd have a horse. But I ended up moving to Los Angeles, and that dream, well, it kind of died."

She reached out a tentative hand towards Sally's nose. The mare edged closer to the door and breathed into Serenity's hand before lowering her head for a scratch. Austin's eyebrows raced towards his hairline again. So far, Sally had only let him touch her. Serenity closed her eyes and smiled as she stroked the mare's long nose.

"She likes you," Austin said.

"Sally's a beautiful horse. Her markings are so unique."

She took her hand away and beamed up at Austin.

"Let's meet a few of the other horses, shall we?"

He stuck out his arm in jest, but she surprised him by threading her elegant arm through it.

"How many horses do you have here?"

"Fifteen so far, but I think we'll be adding more soon. This group over here will be the main stock we use for trail rides."

"Sally's not one of them?" Serenity asked, looking back over her shoulder.

"No, she's one of my personal horses. I brought her with me when I came from my brother's ranch. I found her at auction. She's, well, I guess you could call her my project horse."

"That's nice that Mr. Bohannon lets you keep her here."

"He's a nice man. This is the mare I thought you'd like. Her name's Tilly."

They came to a stop in front of Tilly's stall, and the cute little mare immediately popped her head over the door, expecting to be petted. She was a gregarious little thing who loved attention and treats. Serenity let out a little gasp of appreciation and started scratching behind the bay mare's ears, laughing when Tilly lipped at her sleeve.

"I can already tell this one's a character," she said, running a hand down Tilly's mane.

"That's for sure. She's the friendliest horse I think

I've ever met. Maybe you'd like to go for a ride while you're here? I think you two would get along like cheese and crackers."

Serenity laughed as she kept petting the mare.

"I'd love that. Now I really wish I had different shoes. I should've known a ranch would have horses. It's been years since I've ridden."

Her look of pure delight warmed Austin to his core. He walked to the next horse, a gelding named Steel, and checked his stall.

"Well, now I definitely need to take you out on a ride," he said before moving to the next horse.

Her pretty face flushed, and it felt like the temperature in the barn went up a few degrees as their eyes met. Austin cleared his throat, feeling suddenly awkward.

"If you want to, I mean. It's up to you."

She walked over to Steel and stroked his nose.

"I'd love to. It's important I experience everything the ranch offers so I can write the best article possible."

He dropped his hand to his side. Of course, that made sense. For a second, he'd almost forgotten she was here on a job.

"Let me know when you want to go, and I'll make it happen," he said, trying to be as businesslike as possible.

"Maybe tomorrow?"

"I can have two horses saddled at nine if that works for you?"

"That would be great."

She worked her way through each stall, making sure each horse got a little affection. He watched her honest interactions with the horses. He'd thought she was just a spoiled city girl, but now, in the barn, he could almost picture her wearing jeans and a tee every day. Minus the heels, of course. He laughed to himself and wondered if she was going to appreciate the surprise he had waiting for her in his pickup.

"Is there anything else you have planned for today?"

She walked towards him and nodded.

"I saw some brochures for the local town and wanted to check it out. Do you think I could borrow someone's car and drive in?"

He leaned against a stall and crossed his arms over his chest. It couldn't have been more perfect.

"Actually, I'm done with my duties for the morning. I'd be happy to take you in and show you the highlights. There aren't many, but we could spend a few hours there."

"Are you sure? I've already ruined your morning training session."

"Don't worry about it. Come on, let's hop in the pickup," he said, leaning towards her. "I've got a bit of a surprise for you in there."

Her eyes opened wide, and briefly, he could imagine what she'd looked like as a little girl.

"For me?"

He nodded and motioned for her to follow him as he led the way out of the barn to his pickup. He'd gone into town after dropping her off at the ranch and found a pair of boots he thought were perfect for her. He wasn't sure of the size, but he'd guesstimated and hoped they would fit. He still didn't know why he'd done it, but he felt moved to make the gesture to make up in a small way for their awkward meeting.

He opened the side door and pulled out a bag, turning as she came up behind him.

"For you."

She took the bag and pulled out the box, surprise etched across her features as she opened it.

"A pair of boots? Are you kidding me?"

She pulled the boots out and ran a hand over them with a look of wonder on her face. When he'd seen them at Pete's shop, he thought they'd be perfect for her. Understated and elegant, just like her. The light gray leather felt like butter. She checked the size, and her eyes flew to his.

"How did you know what size I wear?"

"I looked at your feet and estimated. They're okay?"

"Okay? They're amazing," she said, hopping as she took off one shoe.

He grabbed her arm to steady her as she slipped them on.

"Do they fit?"

"Like a glove. Oh my goodness," she said, walking back and forth. "They're so comfortable. You didn't need to do that. I can pay you for them."

He waved her words away like a pesky fly and smiled as he watched her.

"Don't worry about it. I kept the receipt in case I was wrong on the size. You can always exchange them if you don't like them."

"These are perfect."

"Ready to head into town, cowgirl?"

She threw her head back and laughed, a genuine laugh that made his eyes crinkle in the corners. She looked just like a little kid who'd gotten the Christmas present they'd been longing for.

"If my friends could see me now, they wouldn't know what to think."

"Well, I think you look beautiful."

He bit his lip as he realized he'd actually said what he'd been thinking. She paused and dipped her head a little, flushing.

"So, yeah, let's go into town. It's not much, but it's got everything a person needs," he said.

He cleared his throat, feeling awkward as he walked around to the driver's side. Why had that slipped out? He stole a glance at her and breathed in, worried he'd ruined the moment, but she seemed just as happy as she had before. Maybe even a little happier.

"All right, cowboy, let's go."

He chuckled as he fired up his truck. He didn't know how his day had gone from lying in the dirt to taking the prettiest woman he'd ever seen into town, but he wouldn't knock it.

Chapter Seven

Serenity

She propped her head on her hand as she looked out the window, admiring the beautiful views and wide open spaces. She hadn't been sure how she'd feel about being in the literal middle of nowhere, but she surprised herself by feeling quite at home. She glanced over at the handsome cowboy next to her and smiled. When they'd first met, she would've said he was the most obnoxious man on the planet.

Now? She was waffling. She looked down at her feet, and a broad grin stole across her face. The boots were perfect. She never would have thought of buying them herself, but somehow, it was as if they'd been made for her. Austin was bobbing his head to the beat of a country song, and she tapped her toe to the rhythm without even thinking about it.

"You said your brother has a ranch?"

Austin turned his startling blue eyes in her direction and gave her a half-smile that was more ironic than anything.

"Yeah, he's got a spread on the other side of town. It's the family place, actually. When our dad passed away, he inherited it."

Something about the tone of his voice made her look closer at him. His brow was furrowed as he focused on the road ahead.

"Shouldn't it have gone to both of you? I mean, I don't know how ranches work, but it seems harsh that you lived there your whole life and now you're working for someone else."

His hands tightened around the steering wheel, and she bit her lip, worried she'd offended him.

"I didn't mean it like that," she said, reaching a hand out toward him.

"I didn't take offense. It's the truth, after all. I don't know how they do things in the rest of the world, but out here, it's the oldest boy who gets the ranch."

"That doesn't seem fair," she said, interrupting him. "What if the oldest is a girl?"

He quirked a smile, and his face cleared.

"That happens sometimes. But typically, it goes to the eldest boy. I always knew it would happen. I never actually thought of leaving the place, you know? It was home."

"Why did you leave?"

He focused on the road again, and she noticed a little muscle tensing in his jaw.

"My brother and I have different ideas on how to run a ranch. That's all I'll say about it. Things didn't work out, and I figured it was best if I went my own way."

"I see. Well, you seem happy at the ranch. What do you think about it being billed as a haven for the broken-hearted? It's an odd theme for a ranch, isn't it?"

He laughed and shook his head.

"There are worse, I suppose. I like what Mr. Bohannon said about it, though. There's no better place to find your peace than in nature. We've got plenty of that. And there's that old saying, too."

His words tapered off, and a serious look came into his eyes.

"What old saying?" she asked, leaning toward him.

"The outside of a horse is good for the inside of a man. Or a woman," he said with a wink. "I don't want to be sexist. It's true, though. There's something about being around horses that settles a body. Be in the moment. It helps clear your mind."

"I could use that," Serenity said, looking back out the window.

They pulled to a stop in front of a wooden building with a shake roof. The sign looked like it had to be at least fifty years old, and there was something inherently cheery about the bright lights blinking on and off.

"This is the town restaurant, bar, and post office," he said, nodding toward the building. "Did you want to have some lunch? My treat."

She nodded as she slid out of the seat and walked to

meet him in front of the pickup. Her boots rapped on the pavement, bringing a smile to her face.

"I'll have a little something. I had one of Martha's rolls this morning, so I can't eat much for lunch."

She placed her hand over her stomach and winced. He opened the door for her and looked her up and down.

"You look pretty skinny to me. Besides, a place like this really doesn't do diet food."

She snorted and walked past him, waiting as her eyes adjusted to the dim lighting. The savory smell of bacon wafted her direction, waking her stomach up. A pretty girl was behind the bar, mopping up the counter and talking to a customer. She looked up and smiled at Serenity as they approached.

"Hi there. You must be the reporter. I'm Cassie. What can I get you two?"

"Two bacon cheeseburgers, all the fixings, and a pile of your fries," Austin said before Serenity could speak.

She glanced up at him, slightly irritated he'd ordered for her, but she desperately wanted to eat whatever smelled so good. Cassie turned and shouted their order over her shoulder before turning back to them, smiling encouragingly at Serenity.

"Hi Cassie. I'm Serenity Adams, and you've got it right. I'm a reporter. How did you know?"

She sat on a stool next to Austin and put her hands on the gleaming bar top. The old wood gleamed beneath her fingers, and she started tracing the grain.

"A few of the boys from the ranch were in here last

night, and they mentioned you. Hey Austin, how's Jack?"

"His usual moody self. Mind adding a few Cokes to our order?"

Cassie grinned, her freckled nose wrinkling as she filled two glasses with ice.

"Coming right up. You're from California, right?" she asked as she slid a glass in front of Serenity.

"I am. Oh wow, this is good."

Serenity took another long sip of the fountain pop and tried to remember the last time she'd actually had soda. She typically got water with every meal. This was turning into a true treat. She'd briefly promised herself she'd see if the ranch had a gym as she took another sip.

"Thanks," Cassie said, dimpling. "I bet you've got some stories to tell. I'd love to travel someday. Some-times, it feels like I'll be behind this bar for the rest of my life."

The pretty blonde frowned slightly, but it was clear she wasn't a gloomy person as her smile came roaring back.

"But someday, I'm gonna get out there and see stuff. I just know it."

"You will," Serenity said. "Are you from... I'm sorry, what's the name of the town again?"

She looked over at Austin, who'd been watching the two with a smile on his face.

"Granite. It was named for the old rock quarry just outside of town," he said, nodding at her.

"Yep, born and raised, just like this one here," Cassie said, sticking a thumb in Austin's direction. "He was a few years ahead of me in school, but I'm sure I could remember a few stories about him. If you're interested."

Austin blanched and straightened on his barstool.

"I don't think that's necessary..."

"I'd love to hear them sometime," Serenity said, cutting in. "What do you think of the ranch that Mr. Bohannon's building?"

Cassie went back to wiping the counter as she talked.

"He's such a good man. He's done a rare service for this little town. All these new people will come here. It's gonna help a lot of families out. Plus, he's hired a bunch of workers."

Serenity raised an eyebrow.

"Everyone says the same thing about him, that he's a good man. Do you know him at all?"

Cassie stepped back, her open face shuttering.

"Just what people have said. I'll check on your food."

Serenity turned to Austin.

"Did I say something wrong?"

"No, I get that you're curious about Mr. Bohannon. It's just that this is a small town, and we look out for each other. When people ask a lot of questions, hackles go up."

Cassie returned and slid their plates in front of them. Serenity's mouth fell open as she looked at the sheer amount of food piled on it.

"There's no way I can eat all of this," she said, inhaling deeply.

"Do what you can," Cassie said, smiling again. "I can always wrap up what you don't eat for you to finish later. Need anything else?"

"We're good for now," Austin said. "Thanks, Cass."

She nodded and walked down the bar to check in on another customer. Serenity tried to fit the burger in her hands and looked at it with wonder. Where was she going to start? Austin took a giant bite and nodded at her in encouragement.

"Well, here goes," she said, sinking her teeth into the pretzel bun.

The flavors exploded onto her tongue, making her moan aloud in pure enjoyment. Austin's eyebrows went up, and he leaned closer.

"Told you it was good."

She swallowed her first bite and greedily eyed the rest of her burger.

"Good doesn't even do it justice. This is definitely going in my article."

She took a few more bites and kept from moaning out loud again, but it was a near thing. She reluctantly put the burger down and ate a few fries.

"Best place to eat in town," Austin said. "Good thing, too, since it's the only place in town."

She laughed as she swirled her fry into her ketchup.

"Martha mentioned she'd been sending the leftover rolls into town. Where do they go?"

Austin swallowed his bite and took a sip of his drink before answering.

"There are a few families in town that are facing some rough times. I think Martha makes sure everyone has food. She does that with every meal."

"That's so nice. It seems like a genuine community," she said.

"People care about each other out here. I'm sure they do where you're from, but I think it's the pioneer spirit. We've only got each other, you know?"

A sad look crept across Serenity's face as she chewed, thinking about her life in Los Angeles. Sure, she had her friends, especially Lily and Chad. Maybe. But did she really know anyone? Everyone here seemed so close, so caring.

"I like it. The pioneer spirit."

Austin shrugged before polishing off his burger. Serenity ate a few more bites before returning to her fries. Austin made a noise, and she turned to see him smiling. He reached out his hand and raised an eyebrow at her. Confused, she looked at him as he reached out and swiped a little ketchup off the corner of her lip. Her breath caught in her chest as he licked it off his finger. His blue eyes darkened, and she cleared her throat, desperately thinking of something to say.

"I couldn't resist. You looked so cute," he said.

She ducked her head and reached for her napkin, embarrassed. He chuckled and nudged her shoulder.

"Happens to me all the time. Don't sweat it. Well, what did you think of your meal?"

Serenity glanced at her plate, astonished to see she'd finished most of her burger and all of her fries.

"Wow, I can't believe I ate all of that. I'm going to need some extra time in the gym."

"Heck, it's just one little burger."

"And fries."

"Sorry, and fries. You'll be fine."

Serenity made a face and took one last sip of her

drink before looking around the bar. It was a simple place, with a few Western-themed decorations on the walls, but it felt homey and comforting. It was a far cry from the luxurious restaurants she'd been to, but she had to admit that it was one of the best meals she'd ever had. Cassie walked in their direction, a smile back in place.

"I guess I don't have to ask if you liked it," she said, giving Serenity a wink.

"It was amazing. Do you have a website? I'd like to mention this place in my article."

Cassie's eyes shone, and she nodded before reaching under the bar and pulling out a card.

"Here, this has all of our information on it."

"Thanks," Serenity said, tucking the card in her jeans pocket.

Austin stood and pulled out his wallet.

"What's the damage, Cass?"

"I'm buying," she said, nodding at Serenity. "I want to make sure Serenity here feels at home."

Serenity blinked, surprised. Was everyone this nice?

Austin pulled out a ten-dollar bill and put it on the counter.

"Thanks, Cass. You still need a tip, though."

Cassie palmed the ten and put it in her apron, smiling big.

"Appreciate it," she said, turning to Serenity. "Come back any time. Like I said, I've got a few stories about this one you might want to hear."

"I'll do that. Thank you for the amazing meal. It was nice meeting you."

Cassie nodded and took their plates, disappearing

into the kitchen. Austin grabbed a toothpick and fell in next to Serenity as she walked toward the door.

"Where do you want to go now?" he asked.

Serenity walked outside and sniffed the fresh, pine-scented air. The sun was shining, and the sky was that same impossibly blue color that somehow matched Austin's eyes. She looked over at him before turning her face up to the sun.

"You pick."

"All right then. You're in for a tour of Granite's top attractions. Hop in."

They drove for a little while, and he pointed out the school where the local children went, the corner store, and a few unique shops. She looked out the window, charmed by the little town.

"You were right. It's got everything a person needs."

"I know it's not as fancy as what you're used to, but it's full of good people. Sure, we don't have designer boutiques. If you want that, though, Jackson's just a short drive away."

Serenity looked out the window as they drove, feeling charmed by all the tiny houses with their enormous yards. It was the exact opposite of L.A., and it spoke to something deep inside.

"I'd like to get to meet more of the people. Not today, I mean," she hurried to add. "I've kept you long enough. But before I leave…"

"Hey, I don't mind spending time with a beautiful woman," Austin said, giving her another wink. "I'm glad you like the place. Ready to head back to the ranch?"

She flushed at his compliment, feeling her heart squeeze a little. Chad never said things like that to her. In fact, lately, it seemed like they barely talked at all. She shook her head to clear it.

"Let's do it. I told Doc I'd check out his ranch clinic," she said.

Austin didn't respond, and she looked at him out of the corner of her eye, noticing that little muscle in his jaw flexing again. Had she said something wrong? He cleared his throat and forced a smile.

"I see. Well, let's get you back then."

Somehow, the giddy mood had been broken, and Serenity wasn't sure how to put it back together again. They were both quiet as he drove back to the ranch. She thought about and discarded a dozen things to say before they pulled into the ranch yard. He parked the truck and got out without a word.

"Thank you," she said, rushing to catch him. "For the boots, for lunch, for everything."

He tipped his hat at her, and his wry grin was back as his eyes twinkled.

"Any time," he said before turning back to the barn.

She watched him walk away, indecisive. She felt a powerful urge to be near him, even though she knew it was silly.

Chapter Eight

Austin

He headed towards the barn, lost in thought about his lunch with Serenity. She'd opened up, but there was this underlying sadness in her he wished he could heal. Austin shook his head as he grabbed a lead rope from a stall door and headed to the tack room. Why was he so wrapped up in this woman? She was due to leave in a few days, and she had a boyfriend back home. And why was he so jealous of Doc? He'd just spent the better part of three hours with her, but he couldn't get rid of the prickly feeling of jealousy coursing through his veins.

"Um, Austin?"

He popped his head out of the tack room, lead rope forgotten as he heard Serenity's voice echo down the barn's alley.

"I'm back here," he said, ducking back into the room and hanging up the rope. "One second."

Austin walked back down the alley and found Serenity leaning against the doorway of the barn. Her long legs looked fantastic in her jeans, but it was her smile that caught his attention. Her dimple flashed, and his heart skipped a little. He seriously needed to get control of this crush he had on her.

"Sorry to bug you. Again. But would you like to go with me to see Doc?"

"Really? Why?"

He leaned his back against the other side of the door and crossed his arms over his chest.

"If you're not busy, I mean. I know I've taken up a bunch of your time. It's just that, well, I don't know where the clinic is, and I figured we might talk a little more about this place on the way."

His heart tripped again. He wouldn't pass up an opportunity to spend more time with her, even if it meant having to see Doc. Not that he didn't like the funny veterinarian. Well, mostly. He couldn't quite describe the feelings rushing through his chest.

"Of course. It's that building just past the barn, about a hundred yards away," he said, pointing towards the low-slung, modern structure. "But I'll be happy to come with you."

"Well, now I feel like an idiot," Serenity said, flashing a smile. "I should have guessed it was near where the animals are."

"Hey, don't say that. You're new here. Heck, every-thing is new here, besides the house and that old shed over there. Sometimes I'm not sure where everything's at, either. Come to think of it, we should have some signs made. I'll ask Mr. Bohannon about that. It would make the place feel like a little town. Let's go see what old Doc is up to."

"Is that his actual name?" she asked, falling in beside him.

He looked over at her, noticing the way the sunlight picked up the strands of gold in her dark hair.

"You know, that's a good question. I've only heard him called Doc. I suppose he has a name, but I couldn't tell you what it is."

"Interesting. You should have him look at your head. You hit it pretty hard."

He knocked his knuckles against the top of his head and made a face at her, making her laugh.

"I've got a hard noggin. Like I said, I've had way worse hits."

"Still, just in case?"

"Nah. Well, here we are, my lady."

He swept his hat off, even though he felt half a fool for doing it. Whatever it was about this woman, she made him do things he'd never dream of doing with someone else.

She put her hand on the door and paused, looking at him.

"Thanks, Austin. Do you mind coming in with me? I won't take long. I know you have work to do."

He couldn't keep a silly grin from spreading over his face. Now he wouldn't have to worry about Doc flirting with her behind his back. Of course, Doc flirted with every woman he met, and it rarely bothered Austin, but he couldn't help feeling absurdly happy she wanted him to come with her.

"Right this way," he said, pushing open the door. "Hey, Doc, what's up?"

Doc Watts looked up from behind the counter, where he was standing with a bunch of equipment piled on it.

"Getting ready to check the cows in the South pasture for heat," Doc said, coming around the corner and taking Serenity's hand, placing a kiss on it. "And what are you doing this fine day?"

Serenity smiled, but Austin didn't miss the way she firmly pulled her hand back.

"Austin's been showing me the horses, and then we went into town and had lunch."

"Hey, why wasn't I invited?" Doc asked as he shoved his monitors into a bag.

Serenity looked at the devices and raised an eyebrow.

"What are these for?"

"Mr. Bohannon paid for some state-of-the-art monitoring equipment for the ranch's herd. This device will interact with a transmitter on each cow and read for mounting activity."

A blush spread across Serenity's cheeks, and Austin chuckled.

"No need to put it quite that bluntly," he said.

"Oh, sorry, I forgot you were a city girl," Doc said, giving Serenity his patented charming grin. "I'll watch my language."

Serenity flapped an elegant hand in Doc's direction.

"Don't worry about it. I'm here to learn about the ranch, after all. I don't know if I'll put that in my article, but it's good to know there's an actual working herd on the place. Will guests be allowed to interact with the cows at all?"

"Not if I can help it," Doc muttered under his breath.

"What was that?"

Austin crossed his arms over his chest and exchanged a look with Doc.

"He means that well-meaning guests could get in over their heads and get hurt. I think Mr. Bohannon plans to have a few activities where our guests can feel like they're part of a working ranch, but I don't think they'll be allowed to take part in anything dangerous."

"That sounds interesting. Doc, what else do you do here?"

The vet leaned against his counter and looked at Serenity through hooded eyes before giving her a slow wink.

"Anything that needs doing."

Austin cleared his throat, feeling uncomfortable at his friend's tone. What was wrong with Doc today?

"I see. I assume you make sure all the animals are healthy, vaccinations, that sort of thing?" Serenity asked, all business.

She'd pulled herself up straight and crossed her arms over her chest. Austin's admiration for her kicked up another notch. She knew how to handle a guy like Doc, and that made him feel happy.

"Yes, and like I said last night, occasionally stitch up a random rowdy ranch hand."

"How many cattle are on the ranch?"

"We've got about three thousand, give or take. I think Mr. Bohannon is planning to keep quite a few of the calves to keep growing the herd."

Serenity's eyebrows flew up like doves. Austin caught himself staring and intentionally looked away.

"That seems like a lot."

"A place like this with good water and even better grass could support eight times that amount easily. But it's not the primary focus, so I don't think we'll ever have a herd that big."

"Are there any other animals on the ranch?"

Doc quirked a smile and continued packing up his equipment.

"I think Austin houses quite a few barn cats, and there are a few ranch dogs. Hawk has one I know, and I think there are a few others."

Serenity's face lit up, and she turned to Austin.

"Barn cats? I wish I'd seen them when I was there earlier."

"I'll make sure you see them before our ride tomorrow," he said, looking over at Doc.

The handsome vet's face clouded briefly before he shrugged and punched Austin lightly on the shoulder.

"Lucky cuss. Well, I've got to get going. You can look around the clinic, but there's not much here. See you two later."

Serenity stepped aside so Doc could get past her and looked over at Austin once they were alone.

"Any other cool places I should check out? I probably should go back to my room and work on a few things."

"Other than the bunkhouse, there are not too many buildings to look at. I know Mr. Bohannon has a project he's working on building, but it's pretty hush-hush."

Her eyes lit up, and she turned towards him so quickly her shiny ponytail swung over her back.

"Secret project?"

Austin grimaced and took off his hat, folding the brim.

"Dang it, I shouldn't have said anything."

"Could we go by on our ride tomorrow?"

"I don't know. I guess I could ask."

"Are you planning on talking to him today? Mr. Bohannon, I mean."

"Probably not. Sometimes he comes out to the bunkhouse in the mornings and gets us all lined out, but we usually know what we need to do. He keeps to himself. Heck, when you own a place like this, I think you can do what you want."

They walked back out into the sunshine, and he stopped, loving the way the sunlight played over her hair.

"How many cowboys are there again?"

"Ten total. So far, anyway. We'll probably have to hire more people as we grow."

She ticked off her fingers and looked at him.

"I've met you, Doc, Hawk, Colt, and Jack. Who are the others? What are their jobs?"

"You're just full of questions, aren't you?"

"I'm a reporter. It's kind of what I do," she said, rolling her eyes.

They started walking towards the house, and Austin looked around, appreciating the quiet.

"Well, Hawk is kind of our all-around hand. He's young, so he's still learning all the ropes. He helps whoever needs him. Jack, Colt, Wyatt, Kade, Dash, Tex, and Cooper all work with the cattle. And of course, Doc is the vet."

"You're the only one who works with horses?"

"Yep. We've got an older gent by the name of Hank who pitches in a few times a week to help me out, but he doesn't live on the ranch."

"So, all ten of you live in the bunkhouse?"

He nodded his head and gave her a crooked grin.

"We do. We just sleep there, though, so it's not as bad as you'd think. Sometimes, though, I'll admit to looking forward to warmer temps. Once it's nicer at night, I'll be able to sleep in the barn when I need a little quiet."

She let out a whistle and shook her head.

"I can't say I blame you."

They stopped in the ranch yard near the swing set, and Serenity wandered over and took a seat on the smooth wooden seat. She kicked her legs out playfully as she swung back and forth. He leaned against a nearby tree and watched the pure delight on her face.

"So, what do you do for fun in L.A.?" he asked, finally.

She put her feet on the ground and stopped swinging. He cursed softly to himself as the cheerful look faded from her face.

"Well, I work a lot. When I'm on location, I'm usually researching things for my articles, and I don't really do much partying or anything. I'm rarely home, but when I am, I sometimes hang out with my best friend, Lily. We've known each other forever."

"Sounds lonely. What about... what did you say his name was?"

She sighed and shook her head.

"I didn't. His name is Chad. We've been a couple for, I don't know, five years. But I've been traveling for most of that time, so I guess we've only been actually together for a few months."

"What does he do for a living?"

"He's in finance. He works at one of the biggest firms in the country. I guess he's even busier than I am. He takes me to his events when I'm in town. You know the type. Schmoozing with clients, trying to impress them. Before I left, we kind of got into a fight. I guess he doesn't feel like I'm there for him enough. Maybe he's right."

Austin stuck his hands in his pockets and watched her face. She was looking over at the mountain range that sat to the west with a wistful expression.

"It doesn't sound like he's there for you, either," he said finally, looking at the ground.

"I guess sometimes you really don't know people after all," she said so quietly he almost missed it. "Well, I should get to work. Thanks for listening to me rant."

"Heck, if that was a rant, it was a pretty tame one,"

Austin said, holding out a hand for her to grab as she got off the swing.

She huffed out a laugh and turned to walk up the steps.

"Well, I appreciate you listening to me. And the boots," she said, kicking one foot up.

"They look great on you. See you at supper?"

She smiled over her shoulder as she walked in the door.

"We'll see."

The door swung shut, and Austin kicked at a piece of gravel before turning to go back to the barn.

Chapter Nine

Serenity

She sat in her room, trying to focus on the work she needed to get done, but her attention kept drifting back to the barn. Herm had emailed her some edits she needed to make on a piece before it went live on the website, and luckily, they were minor. In theory, it should have taken her just a few minutes to complete the task, but here she was, an hour later, still daydreaming, sitting cross-legged on her opulent bed.

She didn't understand why she felt this way. It wasn't like her to moon over anyone. In the years she'd been traveling, she'd come across plenty of handsome men, but she hadn't thought twice about them, wanting to stay faithful to Chad. Why was she so hung up on this cowboy? Serenity swore softly to herself and dragged her attention back to her laptop.

Once she had her edits done, she felt more centered and grabbed her notebook to work on her piece about the ranch. This was the planning phase of her work, where she'd jot down ideas and experiences so she could pull everything together when she was ready to write. She started making notes about her experience in town. Sure, it was small. Okay, it was tiny. But it had a feeling of community she hadn't experienced in most places. In a strange way, it reminded her of the villages she'd seen in Thailand.

Even though it was a world apart and couldn't be any more different, the people who lived in Granite, and the ones who worked on the ranch, belonged to something greater than themselves.

She tapped her pen on her lip as she thought. Maybe that's what was making her feel all moony and angsty. Even though she had a few close friends, she'd never felt like she had roots before. These people had roots, and they ran deep into the soil, connecting one another with an unbreakable bond. She put her notebook aside and leaned against the pillows behind her, stretching out her legs and trying to get comfortable.

When she'd heard about this place, she'd been interested but skeptical. How could visiting a ranch in the middle of nowhere heal a broken heart? Now she was seeing some of Jim Bohannon's vision. She frowned, wondering about the secretive owner of the ranch. So far, everyone she'd asked had said the same thing. He was a nice man. That was undoubted, but *who* was he? Why did he feel he needed to help broken people heal?

If she could find the answer to that question, she

had a feeling she could write one of the best pieces of her career. Serenity's phone dinged, forcing her into the present. She picked up her phone and saw a text from Mandy Jentry. She cocked her head, trying to place the name before it finally hit her. Mandy worked with Chad. They'd met at an event he'd insisted on dragging her to. She opened the message, curious to see why Mandy was reaching out.

Hey, Serenity. This is Mandy with Trident Financial. I don't know if you remember me, but I thought you should know about this. Sorry to be the bearer of bad news, but you seemed really cool, and you don't deserve this.

Serenity blinked, wondering what she was missing when she noticed a picture file coming through. It took forever to load, and when it finally did, it felt like someone kicked her in the stomach.

It was a picture of Chad, dressed to the nines, at some event, judging from the people standing around in the photo's background. He looked happier than she'd seen him in a long time. Chad had his arm around the waist of a tiny blonde, and he was leaning over to... kiss the woman? Whisper in her ear?

The phone fell from Serenity's hand, and she closed her eyes as hot tears threatened to spill down her cheeks. Was that what he'd meant when he said not to bother coming back for a while? How long had he been seeing this woman? She scrubbed her hands over her face, somehow hoping that she'd fallen asleep and dreamt the whole thing. A quick look at her phone made it clear she was definitely awake.

She typed in a response but paused, wondering what

she should do. Questions were swirling in her head, and her heart demanded answers, but she didn't feel like grilling Mandy, someone she barely knew, to get them. She tapped her fingers on the phone and noticed her hands were shaking. It felt like her insides were made of jello.

She typed in *thank you* and sent the text before she could add anything else. Holding the phone like it was a bomb about to explode, she carefully put it on the table, face down, and put her face in her hands.

She hated crying, despised it, in fact. Invariably, she got a headache, and she had never mastered the art of pretty crying. No, she was more of a snot-all-over-the-place, red-faced, angry crier. Serenity swore softly, determined to stop the flow of tears, but her tear ducts continued on, oblivious. That made it twice in one day she'd broken down, she thought as she wiped her cheeks. It had to be a record.

Well, she laughed to herself; at least if she had a broken heart, she'd come to the right place. She sniffed as her tears slowed and wiped her face again. Serenity knew she'd need to talk to Chad to get his side of the story, but deep down, if she was being honest with herself, she'd seen it coming.

It had been there in the inching away of their closeness over the past few months. He'd been withdrawn the few times she'd been home. Instead of facing it and demanding an explanation, she'd buried herself in her work, asking for more assignments. She knew she should feel shocked, but that was one emotion she didn't feel right now.

Serenity walked over to the window and looked out at the distant mountain peaks. There was plenty of time left before dinner. Maybe she'd go on one of those nature walks she'd seen mentioned downstairs in the lobby. It was better than sitting up here feeling sorry for herself.

She went to the bathroom and made a face when she saw what she looked like in the mirror. Nope, she was not a pretty crier. She grabbed a washcloth and ran cold water over it before pressing it to her hot cheeks. The shock of the cold made her feel absurdly better somehow. She blotted her face a few more times before wringing the water out of the cloth and hanging it on the rack.

There, that was better, she thought as she looked in the mirror. She was still a little blotchy, but who cared about that? She walked over to her suitcase and grabbed a hoodie, tying it around her waist before she walked out of her room. Now, all she needed to do was find a hiking path, and maybe she could outwalk the feelings burbling up in her chest.

As she went down the stairs, she noticed Martha coming up with a man behind her. His face was drawn, and he didn't make eye contact as they passed. Martha nodded as she passed. Serenity gave her a little wave and continued down the steps. It looked like the ranch had another customer. A little sob wanted to work its way up through her chest, but she firmly told it where it could go as she came to the last step.

Luckily, the dining room was empty. She didn't feel like talking to anyone just now and didn't trust her tears to stay put. Everything felt surreal as she walked to the door and looked up at the map of the ranch. She felt jagged somehow, like she was made of finely ground glass. The first trailhead looked like it was just a few yards away from the main house, and she nodded briskly. That's the one she would take.

She walked out of the house and smiled a little as she heard the heels of her new boots scuff on the gravel. They had been one of the most thoughtful gifts she'd received in a long time. She tugged the sleeves of her hoodie tighter and looked for the trail. Her hand automatically went to the back pocket of her jeans, searching for her phone, and she realized she'd left it upstairs, on the bed. She stopped, wondering if she should go get it, but shrugged and kept going. Maybe being without her phone right now was the best thing she could do.

The sign for the trailhead was right where the map said it would be, and she turned to follow the trail. She'd walked for a few minutes when she heard a whine and felt something bump her leg. A small black-and-white dog stood there, with a hopeful expression on its face. She knelt down and ran her hands through its silky fur, prompting even more wagging.

"You must be one of the ranch dogs Doc mentioned," she said as she rubbed its ears.

The dog spun in a circle and barked sharply.

"Well, it's a pleasure to meet you, girl. I don't know your name, but if you'd like to walk with me, you're more than welcome to come along."

The dog grinned at her, tongue hanging out of its

mouth, and barked again, heading down the trail before stopping to look back at her.

"I'm coming."

She walked faster to catch up to the dog, and it fell in beside her, tail still wagging madly.

"You're a nice pup. Are you a working dog, then? Oh geez, look at me, I'm talking to a dog and asking it questions."

The dog barked again, coaxing a laugh out of Serenity.

"Well, I suppose if you talk back, it's okay, then."

They kept walking, and Serenity poured her heart out to the dog. It never left her side, even when a bird exploded out of the grass next to the trail and took off, squawking.

"Wow, you are a good girl," Serenity said, petting the dog on the head. "I always wanted a dog, but with my schedule and living in an apartment, it never would've been fair."

The dog leaned against her leg and looked up into her face, whining.

"Well, maybe while I'm here, you can hang out with me. If you don't have to work, that is."

She looked at her watch and realized she'd been walking a lot longer than she thought.

"We'd better turn back, girl. It's getting late, and the sun's going to go down soon."

She turned, and the dog raced ahead a few feet before turning back and walking beside her again.

"Yeah, I don't know if I'm that excited to get back, but I don't want to be out here in the dark, I know that."

They walked back towards the ranch in companionable silence. As they got closer, she realized how much better she felt than when she'd left. She thought she wanted to be alone, but the little dog had been quite the therapist. She'd shared things she hadn't told another soul and felt lighter than she had in a long time.

"Thanks, girl. For being here for me, I mean," she said, petting the dog again.

The dog's bright brown eyes creased in pleasure as Serenity found an itchy spot on her back. After a few seconds, she raced off, only to turn back, hind end raised up in the air and wiggling playfully.

"I wish I had a toy for you to chase," Serenity said. "I bet you'd like to play fetch."

They walked back into the ranch yard, and Serenity pulled up short, not sure she wanted to face a bunch of people at dinner. Even though she felt better, her emotions were still raw around the edges, and she felt bruised somehow. She looked down and saw the dog was sitting, one haunch planted on the top of her boot.

"What do you say, girl? Still want to hang out with me?"

The dog yipped once and spun around, grinning again.

"All right, let's see what's around the back of the house. I think the map mentioned some sort of meditation garden. That sounds like something I could use right now."

She walked alongside the house, following the gravel path as the dog skipped next to her. As she came around the corner, her breath caught in her throat. Here, in the wilds of Wyoming, was a garden that would put the most elegantly planned park to shame. How had she not discovered this yet?

Green hedges bordered the space, enclosing a riot of early spring flowers. A fountain was in the center, sending up a soothing spray of water. Her foot moved towards a bench across from the fountain, and she sank down onto the seat with a sigh.

The dog surprised her by joining her on the bench and wiggling its nose under her arm for a hug. Serenity closed her arm around the dog, holding it tight as she listened to the soothing rhythm of its breath. They sat there, watching the solar lights flip on one by one as the sun set.

Chapter Ten

Austin

He walked into the ranch house, barely able to contain his excitement over seeing Serenity again. He shook his head as he cleaned his boots. It had only been a couple of hours, and here he was, acting like they'd been separated for years. Satisfied his boots were clean enough to pass Martha's eagle-eyed inspection, he walked into the dining room, surprised to see it was still empty.

Austin headed to the kitchen, following the scent of what he hoped was roast beef. It sure smelled like it, and his stomach rumbled in anticipation. No one was a better cook than Martha, but her roast beef could probably win an international award. He spotted the tiny woman heaving a pan out of the oven and raced over to help her.

"I've got it," she said, plopping it down on the

counter and swatting him with a dishtowel. "You're here early."

"I finished my work for the day. Got anything to snack on?" he asked, eying the steaming platter.

She rummaged around in the fridge and turned around, handing him a carrot.

"Here, stick that in your craw for a little while. It's the only thing that won't spoil your supper."

He snapped off a bite and grinned at her.

"How long until we eat?"

"That roast needs to sit for about half an hour while I get everything else ready."

"Do you need any help?" he asked.

Martha stopped bustling around and looked at him strangely.

"That's the first time anyone around here has offered to help. What's going on?"

Austin's face flushed, and he looked around the kitchen, feeling slightly awkward.

"I know. We just let you do everything, like cook and clean, and we don't pitch in. This is a big place. Once we get more guests coming in, won't it be too much?"

Martha gave him a blank look for a second before shaking her head.

"Well, you're probably right. Mr. Bohannon says he's planning on hiring someone in a few weeks. Until then, I won't pass up an extra hand. If you want to help, you can set the table."

"Yes'm," he said, grinning broadly and heading for the cabinets.

"When you're done with that, I've got something

else for you to do. You know, you could make two trips," she said, eyeing the tall stack he'd put together.

"Two trips are for weaklings."

He picked up the stack and carefully balanced it as he headed back to the dining room. He laid out the dishes and hoped he'd done it right. If not, Martha would certainly let him know. She was a tiny tyrant, but she ran a tight ship and made sure everyone was fed to bursting. He went back into the kitchen, where Martha was busy at the stove, stirring what he hoped was gravy.

"There, that's done," he said, leaning against the door.

Martha stopped stirring and smiled at him, her eyes sparkling.

"That didn't take you long. You might just have found an alternative career path."

"That's me, horse wrangler and dish stacker, extraordinaire."

She snorted and focused back on the stove.

"I have one more thing you could do. There's a guest in the back garden. Would you mind making sure they know it's almost time to eat?"

"Sure thing."

He headed toward the back of the house, wondering who else had checked in today. Austin shrugged as he walked out onto the garden path. He had spent little time back here, but he'd heard it was really pretty at night. He spotted someone in the dark, sitting quietly on a bench, and headed in their direction, pulling up short when he saw it was Serenity.

She looked like a statue carved from marble as she

stared at the fountain. Dizzy, one of his favorite dogs, was cuddled up next to her, and she wuffed softly as he approached. Serenity turned her head, and their eyes met. The smile fell off his face when he saw how much pain was buried in their depths.

"Howdy. Looks like you've met Dizzy," he said, unsure of what else he could say.

She smiled, but it didn't make it all the way to her eyes. He sat next to her on the bench as she looked back at the fountain.

"That's a wonderful name for her. She's a sweet dog."

"Mr. Bohannon got her from the shelter in town. All the dogs here are from the shelter."

She nodded slowly, running her hand over Dizzy's fur.

"I see why everyone says he's a nice man. He sure seems to be intent on rescuing everything he sees."

Austin leaned back, crossing his arms over his chest.

"That's an apt description of him. These solar lights sure are pretty, aren't they? They give everything a soft glow."

She nodded mechanically, and he saw her cheek twitch in the dim light. He wanted nothing more than to wrap his arms around her and hold her tight. He'd never felt this way about a woman before. This strange urge to protect her and take away all her sorrows washed over him, surprising him with its intensity. He reminded himself she had a boyfriend, even if it sounded like he wasn't much of one, and tried to think about something else.

He sat quietly, listening as the sounds from the house grew louder. The rest of the crew must have arrived. No one missed roast beef night. Serenity looked toward the house and sighed, her thin shoulders slumped.

"I'm not very good company right now," she said.

Dizzy let out a low whine and pushed her head under Serenity's hand. Austin laughed softly at the dog's antics.

"I think Dizzy would disagree. Martha sent me out here to let you know dinner's almost ready. It's her specialty; you don't want to miss it."

Serenity ran her hand over her face and tucked a stray hair behind her ear.

"I don't know that I'm up for a formal meal tonight. It sounds like it's going to be pretty crowded."

Austin leaned forward, putting his elbows on his knees, and tried to think of the right thing to say.

"Tell you what. Come on in with me. We'll sit at the end of the table, and I'll keep you company. With everyone there, they won't even notice if you're not feeling chatty. You've gotta eat something."

She let out a shuddering laugh and stood. Dizzy jumped down and spun around in a circle, tongue hanging out of her mouth.

"That's why we call her Dizzy," Austin said as he joined them. "She loves to spin around."

"I love it," Serenity said, perking up a little. "I don't know when I've met a sweeter dog."

"She's really taken with you," Austin said as they walked toward the house. "We can go in the back way if you'd like."

She nodded and wiped under her eyes.

"That's perfect. I'm not really dressed for a nice dinner."

Austin raised an eyebrow and looked over at her.

"I think you look just fine. We're all pretty casual around here, anyway."

He put his hand under her elbow as they went up the steps, and he felt that jolt that had gone through him the first time they'd touched. He took his hand away, fingers curling, as he followed behind her. Dizzy stopped at the steps and thumped her tail, looking hopeful. He watched Serenity walk away and turned to the dog.

"You've got your special kennel to go to with plenty of good food," he said, still feeling guilty as he shut the door. "See you later, girl."

She jumped up and ran toward the front of the house, tail wagging. He shook his head and followed Serenity into the dining room. His ears hadn't deceived him. The place was packed. It looked like every hand had shown up, but there was one man he didn't recognize. Serenity leaned close, her apple blossom scent tickling his nose, and whispered into his ear.

"That's a new guest. I saw Martha showing him to his room earlier."

Austin smiled and nodded at the man, who was wearing a morose expression and looking down at the table. He knew Martha's dinner would go a long way toward cheering the man up. He found a pair of chairs at the end of the table and nodded toward them. Serenity picked the farthest one, and he hurried to pull the chair out for her. He leaned over and whispered.

"It will be okay, I promise."

She shot him a grateful smile. Now that they were in better light, he could see her eyes were red and she looked like she'd been up for two days straight. His heart ached, and he wished they could have a quiet meal together so they could talk.

"Hey, Austin, you get that mare broken yet?"

He turned down the table, spotting Kade, who was wearing his signature plaid shirt and a big grin. The tall cowboy from Washington State always wore a plaid flannel shirt, even in the summer, claiming it kept him close to his Seattle grunge roots. That was also his explanation for his long hair that brushed the tops of his shoulders. He'd been hired a few weeks ago, so Austin wasn't too sure of the man yet, but he seemed friendly enough and knew his way around cattle. Austin shook his head and smiled back.

"Not yet, but I'm getting there."

"Let me know if you need an expert to take over and show you how it's done," Wyatt said.

Austin smirked at the cowboy sitting across from Kade. He was from Idaho and loved to talk about the ranches he worked on there. Wyatt was one of the older cowboys, and he enjoyed teaching everyone new techniques. So far, he'd been a great mentor to Hawk.

"Know any?" Austin said, grinning widely.

"Good one! Hi, miss, you must be the reporter. It's nice to meet you. I'm Wyatt Locke," Wyatt said, nodding towards Serenity.

She managed a smile and nodded her head.

"Nice to meet you, too."

Wyatt raised an eyebrow at Austin, and he shook his head slightly, letting the man know now was not the time for his usual gregarious teasing. Wyatt nodded and turned back to Kade, talking loudly about a heifer who'd tried to break through a fence.

Serenity gave him a grateful smile as Martha came out, holding a platter almost bigger than she was.

"Here you go, everyone," she said, thumping it down in the center of the table.

The next half hour was filled with the sound of clinking silverware and ranch talk as everyone set to work demolishing the delicious roast. Austin looked over at Serenity's plate, noticing she'd only taken a few bites and was mostly moving her food around the plate.

"Don't you like it? I can get you something else from the kitchen if you don't."

"Oh, sorry," she said, dropping her fork. "It's amazing. I'm just not hungry."

He nodded, falling back into silence as they finished their meal. Once again, as soon as everyone was done, Serenity hopped up and started helping Martha clear the plates. Austin joined in, glaring at Kade's quirked smile.

"It's a new thing we're doing," he said. "Martha has enough to do without cleaning up after all of us."

Kade's smile faded as he looked across the table, seeing just how many dishes were around, before joining in to help carry everything to the kitchen.

Serenity took up the same spot as she had the night before, washing the dishes. Instead of talking like they had, though, she was silent as she carefully washed the plates and stacked them up for drying.

"If you need anything…" Austin said, trailing off as he tried to come up with something good to say.

"I'm sorry I'm such a downer," Serenity said. "I just need to go to my room."

"Miss?" Martha said, bustling up to Serenity.

"Yes?"

"Mr. Bohannon said if you wanted to talk to him, to go on up to his office after supper."

Serenity's face cleared, and she smiled at the small woman.

"That's fantastic. I'll do that."

"I'll take over here," Austin said. "There are only a few plates left, anyway."

"Are you sure?" Serenity asked.

Her eyes looked a little brighter, but the dark smudges underneath them pulled at his heart.

"I'm sure. See you tomorrow?"

She cocked her head to the side as she dried her hands.

"For our horseback ride, I mean. Is nine in the morning still okay?"

Her face glowed, and his heart tripped again in his chest. It seemed to get a little electrical charge whenever she smiled.

"Of course, I almost forgot. I'll see you then."

She folded the dishcloth neatly and laid it on the counter next to the sink before leaving. He watched her walk away and got so distracted he forgot the sink was still running.

A hand grabbed the faucet and turned it off before the sink could overflow, and Austin looked up, meeting Wyatt's interested look.

"Want to talk about it?" Wyatt asked.

"Nah, I'm good."

Wyatt leaned against the counter and appraised Austin with a serious expression on his face.

"You know she's leaving in a few days, right?"

Austin's voice caught in his throat, and he nodded, unable to speak. How on earth had Wyatt known what he was thinking?

"Just looking out for you, man. She's a beautiful woman, and it's clear she was raised right," Wyatt said, gesturing toward the other men who were all busy helping Martha. "I'm guessing she's the one who inspired this new outpouring of help?"

"She is."

Wyatt nodded and looked thoughtful.

"It could work, but the odds are low. She's got a job that takes her all over the world. She's from Los Angeles, for crying out loud."

"How do you know all of this?"

"I've got ears. And one of them got talked off today when Doc showed up to check the cows."

Austin felt a stab of jealousy spike through his chest at the thought of Doc talking about Serenity.

"I know she's not from here and not likely to come back. But there's something about her," he said, gritting his teeth.

Wyatt clapped his hand on Austin's arm.

"I know. Those are the ones that hurt the most. You gotta do what's right for you. And her."

Austin nodded slowly as he went back to washing dishes. Wyatt had a point, and even if he didn't want to admit it, the man was right. He was walking on unsteady ground. Maybe he needed to distance himself from her. He stacked the last dish and dried his hands before leaving the kitchen, lost in thought.

Chapter Eleven

Serenity

She rapped on the door of Mr. Bohannon's office, wondering if tonight was the night she'd finally get a few answers to the questions she had. Serenity still felt jagged around the edges, but thinking about work helped. A voice shouted, "Enter," and she turned the knob, walking into the dim room.

"Thank you for inviting me, Mr. Bohannon," she said once she was settled in the chair.

"Please, call me Jim. What do you think of the place so far?"

She paused, looking down at her hands as her mind went in a dozen different directions. What did she think?

"I think you've built something admirable here," she said after a moment. "A genuine community."

"Interesting. I'll admit that wasn't the answer I was expecting."

He pivoted toward her, and she got her first good look at his face. He had kind gray eyes, and his face was ruggedly handsome.

"It's true, though. From the people who work here to the people you're helping in town, there's a strong sense of collectivism that's typically missing in a resort. Sure, you've got places where the workers are happy and create a pseudo-family, but this is something different."

"Hmm. I take it you went into town today?"

"I did. Austin took me after he had me meet the horses. They're wonderful, by the way. I'll be going for a ride tomorrow. Austin offered to show me around the place."

"That's wonderful. What else have you done?"

"I went on a hiking trail today and met one of your ranch dogs. She's a delight."

"Let me guess, it was Dizzy."

"Yes, how did you know?"

"All the dogs we've taken in are special, but I had a feeling she had an intuitive streak. Some dogs do, you know."

"Do they? I hadn't heard that. Oh, I also saw Doc's clinic and learned a little about the cow operation you've got here. It's impressive."

"Thank you."

"So, why did you create a place that was designed for the broken-hearted? I mean no offense, but it's an odd theme for a place to have, especially a ranch. I can't recall another resort that's done something similar. You could've gone with a simple dude ranch, and it would probably be very popular."

He let out a sigh, and Serenity leaned forward, thoroughly intrigued by the mysterious owner of the ranch.

"When people go through a traumatic experience, they're always told to get back on the horse, so to speak. You know the saying: there are so many fish in the sea. Put yourself back out there and find love again. But for many, it's not that simple. A truly traumatic event rips your old life away from you. It doesn't have to be a relationship. There are many ways to get your heart broken."

"Interesting. I think I understand. And you feel that being on a ranch, in the middle of nowhere, can offer healing in a way?"

The chair rocked forward, and Jim stood, keeping his back to her. She noticed he walked with a pronounced limp. He stood in front of the window and clasped his hands behind his back.

"I believe it can. When your life is turned upside down and everything looks bleak, I think the simple things speak to your soul. Wide open spaces, clean air, and things that are out of step with your normal life can be therapeutic. Physical tasks, especially ones that you're not familiar with, do more than take your mind off your heart. They provide an outlet for healing."

Serenity leaned back in her chair, considering his words. Until today, she'd never thought about the way heartache affected more than just your emotions.

"I see what you're saying. If you don't mind me

saying so, it sounds like you're speaking from experience. Is that what made you create this place?"

"You're insightful. I suppose that's an important trait for a writer."

She noticed he didn't actually answer her question and debated whether to press the subject. His breathing had changed, and it almost seemed like he was in pain somehow. Her fingers gripped the arms of her chair in sympathy.

"I noticed a new guest came in today. Do you have a lot of interest in your concept so far?"

He barked out a sharp laugh and leaned harder into the window.

"If there's one thing in this world, it's plenty of heartache. I expect we'll be booked solid soon enough. With God's help, maybe we can help most of them heal. At worst, they'll have a pleasant diversion to take their minds off their pain."

"It's an admirable goal, Jim. I hope you find success."

"Thank you, Serenity."

Her phone chimed, and she apologized as she pulled it out of her pocket. She let out a gasp as she read the message and immediately tucked her phone away, wishing she hadn't seen it.

"Is everything okay?" Jim asked.

While she'd been looking down, he made it back to his chair. She sorted through several replies in her head before answering. Her breath hitched in her chest, and she struggled to keep her voice steady.

"I'm not sure," she said.

"Is there anything I can do to help?"

His voice sounded warm, and she could feel his sincerity.

"I don't know. I honestly don't know what to do right now."

"Are you sure you're okay?"

"I'm fine, thank you. It's... it's been a long day."

"It will be okay. From the sounds of it, you're going through something tough. I'll pray for you tonight."

His words somehow filled her with comfort. She nodded and stood.

"Thank you."

"If you need anything, Martha and I are always here. She's been a loyal housekeeper, but as I'm sure you've seen, she's more than that."

"She's a marvel."

Serenity paused with her hand on the door handle.

"I think you're doing an amazing thing, Jim. I'm looking forward to writing my article on this place."

"Have a good night. It gets better, I promise."

She nodded and walked out, closing the door softly behind her. Her phone felt like it was burning a hole in her pocket. Chad had finally reached out, but his message filled her stomach with turmoil. She pulled the phone out of her pocket and read the text again.

We need to talk. Call me when you get this.

Seeing his name brought back the image of him with his arm around a woman she didn't know. Had he somehow found out what Mandy sent her? She smirked and started dialing his number as she walked back to her room. Only one way to find out.

"Hello?"

"Chad, it's me. I got your text."

His voice, the one she'd gotten so used to, sounded different somehow. Harsh. Unfamiliar. She collapsed onto the bed and kicked off her new boots, placing them carefully by the table.

"Finally. So, yeah, we probably should talk."

"Okay."

He was silent for a beat, and she tried to picture him in her mind. He was probably at home, sitting on their leather couch. To his left was the window that looked out across the skyline of downtown. A skyline she thought she loved.

"Well, it's come to my attention that someone sent you a picture."

"You are correct," she said. "Do you want to explain it? I'll listen if you do."

Silence again.

"You know what? I don't."

"Good enough. They say a picture says a thousand words, I guess," she said, trying to keep her voice from shaking.

"When are you coming back? I'm sure you'll agree we don't need to drag this out. I'd like you to get your things out of the apartment as soon as possible."

"Why? So your new fling can move in?" she asked, hating how angry she sounded.

He sighed, irritation seeping through the phone.

"I don't want to do this. We had a good thing, but it's run its course, you know? Let's not make it ugly."

Serenity's heart started beating faster, and she could

feel an angry flush working its way from her chest to her face.

"Ugly? Seriously? I'm not the one who didn't bother to break things off before starting something new. We've been together for five years!"

"We're not doing this. Come get your things in the next three days, or they're going to the charity shop."

She nearly dropped her phone in disbelief.

"What do you mean?"

"I mean, I want your stuff out. Gone. You know my name's on the lease, so don't even think about trying to say the apartment is half yours."

She looked at the screen on her phone, trying to make sense of what he was saying. Why was he being so nasty?

"Ren? Are you there?"

His nickname for her sounded strange and somehow ugly. She'd always loved it when he called her that, but now it felt like a mockery.

"Fine. I'll come get my stuff."

"I've already changed the locks. The doorman will bring you up, and he'll watch to make sure you only take what's rightfully yours."

He hung up before she could speak, leaving her staring at her phone again. Her hands were shaking, and cold sweat trickled down her back. She punched in Lily's number, praying her friend would answer, but it went right to voicemail. She left a message, not even sure what she was saying, and ended the call. With any luck, Lily would get right back to her.

When she'd seen that picture of Chad earlier, she'd

known they were over, but she never thought it would end like this. Her room felt like it was stifling her, hemming her in. She wiped her palms on her jeans and reached for her boots, shoving her feet in them. Serenity stood, shoved her phone in her pocket, and walked to the door, craving air.

She hurried down the stairs, silently sending up a thank you as she reached the dining room and found it empty. She wasn't in the mood to talk to anyone right now. She walked outside onto the wooden porch and stood there for a second, gulping air and promising herself she wouldn't cry.

She told herself that Chad wasn't worth another tear as she shakily re-tied her hair up into a ponytail. The cool night air soothed her face. She stood there for a few seconds, trying to decide what to do.

"You okay, miss?"

She jumped, startled by the voice coming from her left. The porch light wasn't on, and she couldn't see who she was talking to. She moved closer, letting her eyes adjust, and finally saw Jack sitting there by himself on the porch swing.

"Sorry, I didn't mean to scare you," he said, holding up a hand. "You just looked real upset."

"You could say that."

"Want to head into town with me? I was just thinking about going to the bar."

"I don't know..."

He moved closer and held up his hand again. He had an open face, with kind, deep blue eyes. He clapped his hat back on his close-cropped hair and smiled, putting her at ease.

"I'm not trying to put the moves on you or nothing, miss. I wanted to go to town, but I didn't want to go by myself. If you don't mind me saying so, you look like you could use a drink."

Serenity took a shuddering breath and nodded. She wasn't much of a drinker on a good day, but today had not been a good day. What could it hurt?

"You know what? You're probably right. Just one, though. I need to be up early."

Jack smiled again and held out his arm.

"Let's head in then."

Chapter Twelve

Austin

He lay in bed and looked at the ceiling, wishing sleep would come, unable to think of anything besides Serenity. Should he have said more to her when they were in the garden? She'd seemed so sad, but he wasn't sure if it was his place to pry. He blew air through his nose and flopped onto his side, determined to think about anything else.

It wouldn't be long before they'd be riding the ranch together. He'd already pulled out a saddle he knew would fit her like a glove and gotten everything prepared for the morning. Yeah, it wasn't like he was looking forward to it or anything, he thought, snorting a little. Since the first time he'd met her, he'd acted like a lovesick teenager. He really needed to get a grip.

He listened to the snores coming from the other

cowboys and grimaced. Usually, he was out like a light and never had to listen to Wyatt, who made noises that would put a freight train to shame. He turned onto his other side, determined to block out the noises of everyone else sleeping peacefully.

His phone buzzed on the table next to his bed, and he turned over quickly before it could sound again and wake everyone up. Who on earth would text him at this hour? He squinted at the screen, trying to make sense of the text Cassie sent.

"Can you come into town? Serenity is here, and she's in no shape to go home on her own. Jack isn't either. Again."

He frowned, not liking the spike of jealousy that shot through his chest. Why was she in town, at the bar, with Jack? When he'd last seen her after dinner, she was headed up to talk to Mr. Bohannon. Obviously, something had happened in between then and now, and he wasn't sure he wanted to find out what it was. He sighed and sat up, running his free hand through his hair as he typed a quick reply to Cassie. It was nearly closing time for the bar, and he needed to hurry, or the poor girl would be stuck there way too late.

He quickly dressed, tossing on an old tee and a pair of jeans. The nights were a little chilly, but right now, he felt hot and out of sorts. The cool night air would probably do him some good. He grabbed his keys off the table and walked as quietly as he could to the door.

"Austin? What's wrong?"

"Nothing, Hawk, go back to sleep."

The young cowboy muttered something unintelligible, and Austin laughed quietly as he closed the door behind him. He fired up the pickup and tried not to let his mind run wild.

"Only one way to find out what's going on," he said under his breath as he dialed up his favorite country station.

The drive into town was quick, and he pulled into a spot right in front of the bar. Main Street was completely deserted, minus Jack's pickup in the spot next to his. Austin got out, figuring Cassie must have parked in the back. The bright lights on the bar's sign were out, and he could see just one light on inside the bar. He went through the front door and spotted Serenity slumped over the bar. Jack was a few stools down, with his head buried between his arms.

"Oh good, thank you for coming," Cassie said, looking relieved. "I wasn't sure if Serenity was about to hurl."

"Thanks for that lovely visual," Austin said, looking between the two. "What happened here?"

Cassie slung her purse off the wall and walked over between the two at the bar.

"That girl is going through a nasty breakup, so you be nice to her. From what little I heard, she's been through the wringer tonight," she said, her face softening as she stroked Serenity's hair off her forehead. "This one over here, well, heck if I know what's bothering him lately."

"How many drinks did she have?"

"Two."

He looked over at Cassie with a raised eyebrow. She held up her hand and snorted.

"I never over-serve. Especially after... Well, you know the story behind that one. Seriously, she had two rum and Cokes, and I even went light on the rum. Jack, though, must have pre-gamed. I only served him a few beers."

"Dang it, he drove Serenity here. He should know better. You know how he feels about..."

"Yeah, I know. In a perfect world, it would work out and Jack and I could be together, but I don't know, Austin. There are a lot of hurt feelings. On both sides. We'd both have to change, and I'm not sure either of us is ready for that."

"Well, I won't tell you how to live your life."

"Good, 'cause I wouldn't listen anyway. If you want to take Serenity, I can manage Jack."

"Are you sure? How's he going to get back to the ranch? I don't want him to wake up and try to drive."

"Trust me, it's not the first time this has happened. We've got a routine. I take him to my mom's place and take his keys with me. If he wants to get back in his pickup, he's got to go through me first."

The little blonde smiled and stuck out her chin. She was tough, but he knew under that exterior she was hurting for Jack as much as he was. He didn't know Jack was making this a regular thing. She was right. They needed to have an intervention to help the moody cowboy sooner rather than later. He was going to hurt someone or himself if he kept up his destructive behavior, and Cassie had enough on her plate without needing to look after Jack. Maybe it was time to ask Mr. Bohannon for some advice. Austin put his hand on

Cassie's shoulder. She looked tired, and his heart went out to the pretty girl.

"If you ever need help with Jack, don't be afraid to call me, okay? We've got to do something about him soon. It shouldn't always fall on your shoulders."

"Yeah, I know."

He looped Serenity's arms around his neck and cradled her. She was a tall woman, but she felt as light as a bird as he carried her to the door. Cassie ran after him, holding a bag.

"Here, don't forget this; her phone is in it. She said she turned it off and never wanted to look at it again, but I'm sure by morning she'll need it, especially since she asked me if I had your number. I helped her add it to her contacts."

"Thanks, Cass. For everything."

"Anytime. See you later."

He heard the lock turn as she closed the door behind him. He balanced Serenity as he opened the passenger door and slid her in carefully. He tucked her feet in and smiled when he saw she was still wearing the boots he'd gotten her. As he walked around to the driver's side, he thought about what Cassie had said. As of a few hours ago, Serenity had been in a relationship with that Chad loser, but it sounded like that had changed. He fired up the pickup and headed back to the ranch, thoughts racing ahead of him.

"Where are we?" Serenity asked, her head flopping to the side as she tried to look at him. "Hey, how did you show up? Where's Jack?"

"Cassie texted me. We're heading back," he said. "She's taking Jack to her mom's place."

"That's good. He's a nice guy. I feel bad for him. He really loves her."

"Jack's got some issues that he needs to work out. He and Cassie used to date back in high school."

"That's cool," she said, as her head flopped to the other side. "It's so pretty out here. I love looking at the stars. You know, you can't really see many of them where I live. I always miss that when I go home."

Her voice caught on the word "home," and her shoulders heaved slightly. He looked over at her, concerned, and saw her eyes were closed tight.

"Everything okay?"

She blew a raspberry, and he laughed at the unexpected sound.

"Just peachy. Are we there yet?"

He turned into the ranch yard and pulled up to the house, dousing his lights right away. With any luck, he could get her up to her room with no one hearing.

"We're here. Wait! I'll help you get out."

He was too late. She'd opened the door and spilled out onto the gravel. He cut the engine and dashed around the front of the pickup, coming to a halt when he saw her sprawled flat on her back on the ground. She was laughing like a loon. He grabbed her bag and slung it over his shoulder.

"Are you okay?" he said, kneeling and brushing back her hair.

"I'm amazing. Look, there's Cassiopeia."

She pointed toward the sky, but he looked at her face

instead. She had to be the most beautiful woman he'd ever seen, and he hated seeing her hurt. He took her arm and helped her to her feet as she swayed back and forth.

"Geez, if this was the product of two rum and cokes, I'd hate to see what would happen with three," he said under his breath as he guided her toward the walkway.

"Hee, that's funny," she said before halting. "Oh, no."

"What?"

"I don't feel so good."

She lurched to the side and knelt on the grass, holding onto the dirt with both hands as she threw up. Austin closed his eyes and shook his head, determined not to give in to a sympathetic reaction to do the same thing. He knelt next to her and smoothed her hair as she emptied her stomach.

She backhanded her mouth and rocked back on her heels. He heard footsteps on the gravel and turned as Dizzy approached, tail wagging. He steered the dog away from the mess on the grass and helped Serenity stand again.

"Let's get you inside."

She felt boneless as she leaned into him, and he scooped her up in his arms again, figuring it would be easier to carry her.

"Hey, Austin. You're cute," she said, way too loud, as they walked inside.

"Shhh, we don't want to wake everyone up."

She held her finger to her lips and shushed him back. He smiled as he navigated the stairs, hoping he wouldn't trip. She couldn't have weighed much, but the stairs seemed to stretch on forever.

Once he got upstairs, he found her room, flipped on the light, and gently put her on the bed. Her room was tidy, and it looked like she hadn't even unpacked. His heart gave a brief twinge as he saw her bag. She'd been leaving all too soon. He felt a tail smack his leg and looked down.

"Dizzy! How did you get in here? You know you're not supposed to be inside."

The small dog looked up at him and jumped on the bed, curling up next to Serenity and nosing its head under her arm.

"Such a sweet doggie," Serenity said, so quietly he almost didn't hear her. "You're sweet, too. Sweet and hot, what an impressive combination."

He smoothed her hair again and gently removed each boot. He remembered her bag and put it on the table.

"Hey, Austin, c'mere," she said, holding out a hand towards him. "I wanna give you a kiss."

He took her hand, kissed it, and folded it over her chest.

"Tell you what, I'll take a rain check on that. You need to get some sleep."

She curled on her side, cuddling Dizzy as she rubbed her cheek on the pillow.

"K, g'night."

Her face relaxed, and she was out like a light within seconds. He looked at her as she slept, lashes fanned across her pale cheek. She was going to be a hurting unit in the morning. He walked into the bathroom and searched through the medicine cabinet, hoping it was stocked for the guests. Sure enough, he found a bottle of aspirin. He grabbed that and filled a glass with some water, putting them both on the table next to the bed.

"Watch over her, girl," he said to Dizzy.

He heard her tail thump once on the bed as he turned to leave. His feet stopped as he took one more look at the bed.

"Good night, Serenity."

He saw her mouth twitch into a smile before he turned the light off and shut the door. The clock in the entryway chimed softly as he hustled down the stairs. It was going to be an early morning, but he was glad he'd been able to see her safely home. He kept hearing her say she thought he was cute as he got back in his pickup and drove over to the bunkhouse. Did she really feel that way? He walked into the bunkhouse, took off his jeans, and got into his bed, trying to make sense of all his feelings until sleep finally claimed him.

Chapter Thirteen

Serenity

The muffled sound of a phone ringing finally roused Serenity several hours later. She sat up in bed, regretting her quick movement instantaneously. By the time she realized where she was, who she was, and that her phone was in her bag on the table by the bed, it had quit ringing.

She lay back down, wondering if it was worth it to dig her phone out and see who called. A soft whine caught her attention, and she looked down, noticing the dog curled up next to her.

"Dizzy? What on earth are you doing here? What happened last night?"

The dog licked her hand as Serenity tried to put all the pieces together. The phone call with Chad. Going to the bar with Jack and talking with Cassie. From there, everything was blank. Her phone rang again, and she rubbed the top of Dizzy's head.

"I guess I'd better get that, huh?"

She reached over and grabbed her bag, wincing at the movement, and spotted the glass of water and bottle of aspirin next to it. Well, that solved the mystery of how she'd made it back here, she thought as she grabbed her phone. But who brought her? Whoever they were, they were certainly thoughtful. She glanced at the screen and hit the accept call button.

"This is Serenity," she said, shaking out a few aspirins into her hand.

"Where have you been? I've been trying to reach you for the past hour," Herm said, barking at her through the phone.

She winced again and swallowed the aspirin with a gulp of water before answering her boss.

"Time zones, Herm. It's still dark here," she said, squinting at the window.

"Oh... right. Anyway, I wanted to follow up on your story. How's it going out there in the wild west?"

"It's been... wild."

"You've got some good stuff for your piece?"

She took another drink of water and leaned back against the pillows as Dizzy licked her hand and thumped her tail on the bed. She hoped she wouldn't get in trouble for having the dog in the room with her, but then again, she hadn't been the one to let her in.

"I do. I'm supposed to go for a trail ride today to view the rest of the ranch. A ranch hand named Austin will take me."

Mentioning his name brought back a flood of memories. Him carrying her to his pickup, her throwing up in the yard (and oh God, she'd probably need to clean that up), and worse, a wisp of a memory of asking him if she could kiss him. Him tucking her in and being the perfect gentleman. She groaned and put her forehead in her hand.

"Then again, that might not happen," she said, not knowing if she could face the handsome cowboy again.

"What do you mean? That would be great. Make sure you get a bunch of pictures. When are you scheduled to come back?"

"Two more days, but I'm going to bump that up to tomorrow, I think. I've got everything I need."

"Better check and make sure you can get a flight. I don't know how often planes fly out of there."

"Don't worry, I'll make it happen."

"Serenity, is everything okay?"

She snorted and looked at Dizzy, who was lying on her back, all four legs in the air, tongue lolling out of her mouth in a silly grin. Serenity rubbed the dog's tummy and smiled to herself.

"All things considered, I guess they could be worse. Marginally."

"Well, you know what I always say: focus on your work, and everything else will work itself out."

That's exactly what she'd been doing for the past two years, and she wasn't so sure it was a good thing. She wasn't about to tell her editor that, though.

"Sounds good, Herm. I'll text you when I have a flight booked. See you soon."

"Stay safe."

Herm ended the call, and Serenity started checking through her notifications. Nothing more from Chad, but that was probably a good thing, considering what happened the night before. She blew her hair out of her face with a sigh. Lily had tried to call and text.

What's up, girl? Why won't you answer your phone?

Serenity tapped her lip with her finger and debated calling or texting her friend back. Figuring it was a conversation best done in person, she tapped out a quick text.

Lots going on. Mind if I stay with you tomorrow night? I'll be flying back in the morning.

That reminded her she needed to see if she could book a flight. She tapped open her browser and searched for flights from Jackson to Los Angeles. There was one leaving early the next day. She glanced at Dizzy, already missing the sweet dog, as she booked the flight.

"Well, that's done. I guess I'd better get ready to face the day. And Austin."

Dizzy stayed on the bed, content to lie on the soft mattress while Serenity got ready. She brushed her teeth, grimacing at the horrible aftertaste in her mouth, before jumping in the shower.

The hot water helped, but she figured it was the aspirin kicking in more than anything as she finished getting ready. She tossed her wet hair in a ponytail and skipped her makeup. After last night, Austin had already seen her at her worst. She highly doubted adding eyeliner and blush was going to make him forget the way she'd acted the night before.

"Ready to go, Dizzy?"

True to her name, the dog hopped off the bed and spun in place before letting out a bark and rushing for the door. Serenity laughed as she hurried to get her boots on. Her hand touched the soft leather, and she smiled briefly before opening the door to let the dog out of her room.

The man she'd met on the stairs was in the dining room, talking with Martha, as she hit the bottom of the stairs and headed for the door. Even though the food on the table smelled delicious, her stomach rebelled at the thought of eating anything just then.

She opened the front door, and Dizzy raced off, tail wagging. Serenity checked her watch and nodded. She still had half an hour before she was supposed to meet Austin, but she figured she may as well get it over with. He was kind and gentle with her, making sure she was taken care of. It had been a long time since someone had treated her like that. She glanced at the corner of the yard where she thought she'd lost her cookies, but luckily, she saw nothing.

As she walked over to the barn, she thought back to her past relationships. If she was being honest, no one had ever treated her like that. She'd dated on and off through college, but they were all similar—so similar they blurred together a little in her memories. She shook her head as she walked into the barn. Considering how things with Chad had ended up, she was losing confidence in her ability to pick the right man.

"Hello?"

"Howdy, miss."

Serenity smiled as an older man came around the corner carrying two buckets. He nodded and smiled, revealing a few missing teeth.

"You must be Hank. Austin mentioned you yesterday. Is he around?"

"He'll be in the back with the kittens this time of the morning. He always checks on them to make sure they're okay," Hank said, nodding his head in the direction she should go.

"Thanks."

She walked down the barn aisle, stopping to pet the horses that had popped their heads out to greet her. The warm smells of the barn made her feel somehow at home, and she realized just how much she'd missed being around animals. She'd love to include them in her life. Her smile slipped as she realized how difficult that would be, especially now that she didn't have a place to call home.

Serenity kept walking to the end of the aisle and turned right, hearing Austin's voice.

"You're a feisty little one, aren't you?"

The smile came back as she entered the small room at the back of the barn. Austin was crouched down, holding onto a kitten that was batting him in the face. He looked up as she entered, and she blushed as their eyes met.

"Good morning."

"It's a beautiful one. Want to hold this little tiger for me?"

Austin handed her the warm kitten, who snuggled into her hands, tiny whiskers tickling her skin. She used a finger to brush its head as it rumbled out a loud purr.

"Aren't you just adorable," she said, pressing the kitten to her chest. "How many are there?"

Austin glanced over at her as he dug around in the stacked hay for another kitten.

"Gotcha! Just three in this litter. We're going to have Doc spay the mama as soon as she's done nursing. She was a stray who showed up about a month ago. Once these little guys are old enough, we'll do the same thing with them."

"Where's the third one?" Serenity asked, looking around Austin's broad shoulders.

"I think he's... yep, he's right here," he said, grabbing another kitten from behind the bale. "That's all of them."

The kittens were as different as night and day. The one in Austin's arms was a bright orange tabby, while hers was dark black. The kitten sitting on the bale was a mix of black and white, with an adorable white mustache on his black face.

"They're precious."

"All life is. We'll probably let them stay as barn cats, unless we can find someone who wants to adopt one. They'll be well cared for here, though."

"I wish I could adopt one," she said, holding her kitten up so she could see its little face. "I've always loved black cats."

"She likes you," he said, watching the kitten try to snag a piece of Serenity's ponytail.

"About last night... I, well, I understand if you want

to cancel our ride this morning," Serenity said, focusing on the kitten so she wouldn't have to look at Austin.

"Why would I want to do a crazy thing like that?" Austin asked.

"Well, I don't know. I just..."

He tucked the kitten in the crook of his arm and walked closer to Serenity. He tucked a stray hair behind her ear and smiled at her.

"Hey, don't worry about it."

He lifted her chin and focused back on the cat in his arms. Serenity felt her heart constrict as she watched him play with the kitten. He was such a kind person once you got to know him. She smirked, remembering her first impression of him. She'd thought he was a cocky know-it-all, but he was a man who truly cared about animals and treated her with respect. Tears threatened to well in her eyes, and she blinked hard.

"I appreciate it," she said as she put the kitten down next to its brother. "Where's their mama?"

"I expect she's out there hunting. Or she just needed a few minutes away," Austin said with a laugh. "I can only imagine what taking care of these three yahoos is like. She'll be back in a little while. Ready to get saddled up?"

She nodded, and he placed the other kitten along-side its siblings before offering her his hand. She slipped her hand into his and felt a warmth course through her soul. She almost regretted booking that flight, but she knew she couldn't stay here indefinitely. As nice as it was being surrounded by wide open spaces and all the critters she could ever want, real life was waiting back in California. It wouldn't be pretty, but she knew she needed to deal with it.

"Let's go."

He led her out of the room and closed the door, leaving it open a crack for the mama cat to return.

"I've already got Tilly and Steel ready to go. Where did you want to go first?"

She shrugged her shoulders as she followed him into the corral next to the barn.

"You take the lead."

He winked at her and tipped his hat slightly as they walked up to the horses. Tilly turned her head and whickered at Serenity, nosing for a pet. She stroked the horse's soft nose as she looked at the gear Austin had assembled.

"You're packing heavy," she said, noticing he had saddlebags thrown behind his saddle.

"Well, you never know if we'll come across some fence that needs to be fixed. Need a leg up?"

She nodded as she grabbed the saddle horn and felt his firm hand on her shin. He helped her swing her leg over the saddle and checked the girth to make sure it was tight before stepping back.

"We'll start off slow," he said. "Give you a chance to get used to riding again."

She nodded as she untied the reins from the horn, feeling that familiar joy spring up inside her. It had been too long since she'd ridden a horse. She was used to an English saddle, and this Western version felt more secure. She squeezed her legs around Tilly's sides, and the horse obediently moved off. Austin jumped on Steel and nodded as he trotted past, taking the front position as they left the corral. Hank was there to open and close the gate, and he gave Serenity a big smile as they left.

"Hank's sure nice," she said once they were away from the barn.

"He's a hard-working man, that's for sure. He always beats me to work on the days he's scheduled, and he's usually the last one in the barn."

"Does he live in town?"

"I think he's got a little place in between here and town, but you know, I'm not exactly sure. I'll have to ask him. Ready to go a little faster?"

She nodded and gave him a wild smile as she put her heels into Tilly's side. The little mare immediately shifted into a smooth gallop. Serenity whooped a little as they got going and put her face into the wind, loving the way it made her ponytail stream out behind her. Austin galloped up beside her before pulling away. She spotted his grin as he passed, and she leaned forward, encouraging the mare to go faster.

After a few minutes, they slowed to a trot, and Serenity took in the day's beauty. There was something about riding horseback that made the rest of the world slip away into a distant murmur you could hardly hear. She wished she could make all of her worries disappear that easily.

They came to a stop in front of a building site, and her breath caught in her throat. A cute little cottage looked like it had sprung right out of the prairie.

"What's this place?"

"That's Mr. Bohannon's secret project I was telling you about. I'm not sure I should show you this, so let's keep it between us, okay?"

"It's amazing," she said, swinging her leg off of Tilly to dismount.

She walked around the perimeter of the framed house and imagined what it would look like when it was finished. The windows would look right out to the distant mountain range, and the beginnings of a porch were taking shape. She could imagine what it would be like, sitting here after a long day, taking in the sights and feeling the quiet of the wilderness seep into her bones. It would certainly differ from her current life.

Sadness filled her heart as she walked back to rejoin Austin and the horses. She'd probably never see the little house completed. She remembered Herm's request for pictures and took a few of the surrounding countryside and one of the house, just for herself.

"It's so cute," she said.

"It is nice. I'm not sure why he's building it out here, but he mentioned there'll be a dirt road that will link it with the ranch house and the other buildings. Maybe it's going to be a guest retreat. Need help getting back on Tilly?"

"No, I've got it," she said, swinging up into the saddle. "If I was going to stay here again, this would be the place I'd pick. It's too bad I have to leave."

His face fell, and the cheerful mood they'd shared disintegrated. She looked out across the open range and took a deep breath.

"Ready?"

Not trusting her voice, she nodded and fell in behind Austin as they rode back to the ranch.

Chapter Fourteen

Austin

Austin checked his watch as he headed for the barn much earlier than he usually did. The sun was just peeking over the horizon, washing everything with a dusty glow. He kicked a rock as he walked, frustrated that he hadn't seen Serenity since their ride. She'd been in a good mood until they'd seen the house. He still wasn't sure what Mr. Bohannon was doing with that place. He'd have to ask a few of the other hands to see if any of them had heard anything about it.

Serenity hadn't shown up for dinner the night before, and when he asked Martha about it while he was helping her do the dishes, she'd told him of Serenity's plans to leave the next morning. Martha had already volunteered to drive her, and she shook her head when Austin offered to go in her place.

So, here he was, up before dawn, hoping to get one last glimpse of Serenity before she left—left the ranch, most likely for good. His heart gave a painful lurch as he thought about a life without the pretty reporter in it. They'd only known each other a few short days, but he felt like he was connected to her. He lifted his eyes to the sky and tried to find the words to pray, but coherent thought eluded him. All he could manage was *please*, and he was sure God would understand.

He stopped at the barn doors, uncertain of what his next move should be. There was always plenty to do at the barn, but his boots wanted to turn towards the ranch house. He looked around for Hank, hoping for a distraction, but couldn't find him. This was probably the first time he'd beaten the older man to work. That was one for the record books.

Austin's eyes tracked towards the ranch house again, and he scuffed his boot in the dirt. Martha hadn't said what time she was leaving, but he was certain it would be early. Most of the flights that left the local airport departed before nine. A thump on his leg caught his attention, and he looked down into Dizzy's dark brown eyes. She leaned against his leg and looked up at him mournfully.

"Yeah, I'm going to miss her, too," he said, ruffling the dog's fur. "I don't know what we can do about it, girl."

He heard the ranch door bang and started walking towards the sound without even meaning to.

"C'mon, Dizzy. We can at least say a proper goodbye."

The little dog rocketed out of the barn, barking her head off. He followed behind, wishing he could run with her, knowing it wouldn't be dignified, yet hardly caring. Serenity's silky brown hair streamed down her back, and his heart caught again as he saw her drop her bag and embrace the little dog. By the time he reached them, Dizzy had jumped up and was licking Serenity's face. Her laugh touched him, and again he wished he could be the one to make her laugh, to make that dimple wink, and chase the sadness from her heart.

"Dizzy, don't maul her," Austin said, looking around for Martha.

He spotted Martha's car backing out of the garage and felt his stomach clench. He was running out of time.

"She's fine," Serenity said, wiping her cheek before giving the dog another hug. "I'll really miss her."

"She's going to miss you. She took a rare liking to you. We'll all miss you."

She was quiet as she stood and looked Austin in the eye. Her soft brown eyes looked wounded in the morning light.

"This has been an incredible experience," she said, lowering her eyes. "I'll miss all of you, too."

"I would've taken you to the airport," he said, leaning against the gate as Martha pulled around.

Bless her heart, she looked like she was taking her sweet time getting the car parked.

"I know, but you're busy here. I can't keep taking you away from your work. Could you tell Sally and Tilly bye? And Shadow?"

"Sure, I'll do that. Who's Shadow?"

Her cheeks colored, and she looked off into the distance at the mountains. He leaned closer to catch her answer.

"That's what I called the little black kitten. She was so sweet. I always wanted a black cat named Shadow."

Her words caught, and she cleared her throat, straightening as Martha came around the back of the car.

"Thanks for everything. I mean it. I had a unique time at this ranch," she said, glancing down at her feet. "I hope you don't mind if I keep the boots."

"They're yours. I hope you'll wear them and think of this place."

She nodded, and he picked up her bag, stowing it in the trunk. Dizzy ran in circles around her legs, almost making her trip. She giggled at the dog's antics and knelt down to pet her.

"You be good, Dizzy girl. Thanks for being there for me."

He looked at Martha, and the little woman narrowed her eyes at him before nodding sharply and getting in the car. Austin searched for the right words to say, but they dried up in his throat as he looked at Serenity. She looked like an angel as the morning sun hit her hair, turning the light brown strands into a halo sparked with gold.

Their eyes met, and she took a half step in his direction. He cleared his throat, feeling uncharacteristically awkward.

"So..."

They spoke at the same time, and he laughed, feeling like he was back in a middle school mixer, about to ask a girl to dance.

"If you ever need anything, I'm just a call away," Austin said.

She bit her lip and nodded before turning away to get in the car.

"Wait..."

She turned, and he stepped forward, erasing the gap between them, and took her in his arms. She gasped slightly before relaxing. He closed his eyes and kissed her, feeling a swirl of emotions he couldn't quite name as her lips met his. He deepened the kiss, feeling the shock of her touch rocket to his very core. They separated, breathless, and he blinked hard before meeting her eyes again.

"I'll never forget you," Serenity said as she got in the car. "Take care of Dizzy."

She closed the door and fastened her seatbelt, and before he could think of anything else to say, she was gone. Martha might have been old enough to be his grandma, but she had a lead foot that would put most NASCAR drivers to shame.

The dust settled as the car left the ranch yard, and he raised his hand, hoping Serenity was looking back. Dizzy sat at his legs, leaning heavily against him.

"I know, girl. I feel the same way."

He walked back to the barn, forcing himself to focus on what he needed to do that day instead of thinking about the woman he just might have fallen in love with.

In a few hours, she'd be rocketing towards Los Angeles, and he might never see her again.

His stomach felt like a brick as he walked down the barn's alley, mechanically petting the horses as they came forward to say hello. He stopped in front of Tilly's stall and leaned against the gate. The friendly mare stuck her head out and whickered softly as he stroked her nose.

Serenity had only been at the ranch for a few days, but suddenly, everything reminded him of her. How was he supposed to go on? He shook his head and pulled himself together. He'd need to check on the kittens and get ready to do his morning chores before getting Sally back in the corral for another lesson.

He shoved his hands in his pockets and walked towards the back room. Dizzy fell in beside him, looking lost.

"Are you good with kittens?" he asked the dog as they walked. "You'll have to be real gentle with them, okay?"

He snorted as they walked into the kittens' room. He'd been without Serenity for a few minutes, and he was already talking to the dog like he expected her to answer him. A chorus of mews started up as he walked in, and three balls of fluff hopped in his direction, pulling up short when they caught sight of Dizzy. They skittered around the floor, diving behind the hay bales, hissing like crazy.

He glanced down and saw that Dizzy had dropped to her belly and was crawling towards the kittens, wanting to play. The black kitten poked her head around the bale and was currently taking tiny steps towards the dog, fur fluffed up as much as it could go.

Dizzy whined, and the kitten stopped, tottering on its legs before approaching again. The dog put her nose down, and Austin watched as the kitten approached slowly. She reached her nose out to the dog just as Dizzy gave her a big lick. The kitten tumbled backward and scooted a few feet away before bounding towards the dog again, back arched.

He laughed, watching the two interact, and noticed the other two kittens were nervously approaching. Dizzy nosed the black kitten, and it walked forward until it was between her front legs, curling up and cuddling close.

"Dizzy, meet Shadow."

He made sure the cats had fresh food and water as Dizzy gave each one a bath. He wasn't sure the kittens appreciated the soaking, but they seemed pretty happy.

"All right, Dizz. I've got to get to work. Do you want to come with me, or stay here? Watch out for the mama cat when she comes back."

Dizzy's tongue lolled out as she rolled on her back, allowing the kittens to climb up on her chest.

"Well, that solves that. I'll leave the door open for you."

He walked back into the alley and snorted at himself again. Yep, he'd officially gone around the bend. He spotted Hank carrying fresh water for the horses and hurried to the man's side.

"Good morning, Hank. How's it going today?"

"Tolerable, Austin. Tolerable. Where's that pretty girl who was here yesterday?"

Austin swallowed hard and looked away.

"She left."

"That's a darn shame. I liked her. Well, I suppose that's how it's going to be, working for a place like this. People will come and go, and you can't let yourself get too attached."

Hank gave him a keen look and nodded sharply before walking into a stall. Austin kept walking, trying to tell himself the man made sense. If this place took off, and it looked like it would, there might be hundreds of people visiting the ranch in a year. But none of those people would be Serenity.

He'd dated plenty of women in his life, he thought as he went to fill up a few more buckets of fresh water. Heck, he'd probably dated too many. He'd never felt this way about a single one. In fact, if he really thought about it, he couldn't remember most of the girls' names.

Water spilled over the side of the bucket, and he cursed softly to himself as he shut off the stream. He wouldn't get much done if he kept mooning over a woman who'd left. He needed to focus on his job and stop thinking about Serenity. He snorted, remembering her soft lips and the way she'd looked that morning. Not thinking about Serenity was going to be one of the hardest things he'd ever done.

Chapter Fifteen

Serenity

The hum of her office faded into the background as Serenity looked out of her window across from her desk. It had been two weeks since she'd left the ranch, and somehow, she still expected to see blue skies and mountains outside. Instead, she had tall buildings that blocked the sun and gray smog that seemed to settle everywhere she looked.

She pushed away from her desk and leaned against the windowsill, trying to make sense of her life. As soon as she'd come back, she'd instructed her Uber driver to take her to what used to be home. She'd almost wished Chad would have been there so she could confront him, but in hindsight, it was better that he'd been gone. She piled her few possessions into some totes, loaded everything into the waiting car, and went straight to Lily's place.

Her friend lived in a spacious loft apartment, financed in large part by her work as an influencer. She snorted and turned away from the window. Serenity still couldn't believe her beautiful best friend was known around the world. Lily had tried to persuade Serenity to join social media and create a following by posting pictures of the exotic locales she visited, but she couldn't bring herself to do it. It was fine for Lily, who enjoyed being in the spotlight, but for Serenity, it would've been too much.

She walked back to her desk and checked her assignment folder, hoping for something, anything, to take her mind off the wreck of her current situation. It was, unfortunately, empty, and she'd run out of things to occupy her mind. She closed her laptop and slipped it into her bag, ready to head to Lily's place and crash for the evening.

Some delivered food and a night of Netflix sounded pretty darn good right now. Serenity shut off the light in her office and nodded to her co-workers as she headed to the elevator. She was due to take a big assignment in a few days that would take her to Iceland, but somehow, even though it was a place she'd always wanted to go, she couldn't get excited.

She rode the elevator down and looked at her distorted reflection in the metal doors. She'd pursued her goal of becoming a travel writer with a single-minded intensity. While she'd achieved that and more, for the first time in her life, she felt hollow. She shook her head as she walked through the lobby onto the crowded sidewalk. Here she was, literally living her dream, and it depressed her. She came to a sudden halt as a realization washed over her. It wasn't her dream anymore.

Someone bumped into her, and she forced her feet to move again. Lily's loft was only a few blocks away from the magazine offices, and she felt like walking to clear her head. The sea of humanity that was the city she loved felt like it had its own pulse as she walked, and for the first time, she felt like she was out of sync, her heart beating to a far different rhythm. If she was being honest with herself, it had felt that way since she'd gotten on the plane and saw the mountain range that flanked the ranch receding in the distance.

Her hand went to her lips as she thought about the kiss Austin had given her before she'd gotten in the car with Martha. In all her years, she'd never been kissed like that. The ride to the airport had been quiet as Martha focused on the road. The little woman could hardly see over the dash, and Serenity chuckled at the memory. Everyone at the ranch had been so real. Here, she felt like everyone she came into contact with was fake.

She mindlessly walked up the steps to Lily's place, remembering Dizzy, the horses, and the adorable kittens. And Austin. How could she forget those amazing blue eyes and his gentle ways? She used the key Lily had given her and walked in, tossing her bag onto the side table by the door.

"Hey, pretty lady. You're home early," Lily said as she poked her head around the corner.

Her gorgeous red hair was piled on her head, and she was wearing elaborate makeup.

"I finished up my work for the day and thought I'd come back and drown my sorrows in some pad Thai and mindless scrolling through Netflix."

Serenity detoured to the kitchen and grabbed a bottle of water from the fridge. She turned around and saw Lily looking at her with an expression she couldn't quite read.

"You know what? I feel like staying home, too. What do you say we have a girls' night?"

Serenity coughed as she tried to laugh while swallowing.

"Minus the robe you're wearing, you don't look like you're ready for a night in. It's fine," she said, flapping her hand in Lily's direction. "You should go out and have some fun instead of hanging out with your resident wet blanket."

"Whatever. I've been running non-stop for weeks. We need this. Tell you what, go take a nice bubble bath, and while you're soaking, I'll order up some food, and it will be here by the time you get out. We can have a regular girl-talk session."

Serenity downed the remaining water and tossed the bottle into the recycling bin.

"That sounds like fun. I won't take long."

"Take all the time you need. Oh, do you want some mango sticky rice?"

"Do I ever say no to that?"

They shared a laugh as Serenity walked back to the corner Lily had designated as her guest space. A dividing screen gave her a sense of privacy, but she still wasn't quite used to the whole open-concept thing. Thankfully, the guest bath was closed off, and she shut the door and leaned against it, fighting her emotions.

As she ran the bath, she sorted through the crazy amount of bubble bath options her friend stocked on the shelves above the tub. After picking a vanilla-scented one, she poured in a generous dollop and waited for the tub to fill before sinking in.

Thoughts of Austin crowded into her head, and she tried to blank her mind, determined to focus on absolutely nothing while she soaked. It worked for about three minutes before she thought of his kiss. Her toes curled involuntarily at the memory.

Frustrated, she drained the tub, dried off, and threw on the robe that was hanging by the door. As she walked into the living room, she heard the security panel chime and saw her friend dashing toward the door.

"Perfect timing, as always," Lily called over her shoulder before opening the door.

Serenity sank onto the padded leather couch and looked out the floor-to-ceiling window that flanked the living area. From up here, the city didn't seem as grungy, but she still didn't have that same feeling in her chest she used to get when looking at the buildings and lights.

"Here you go," Lily said, plunking the bag down on the coffee table. "Let's dig in!"

They sorted out their food orders before Lily scrolled through the Netflix lineup, making faces at a few titles.

Serenity's spirits rose as they talked and laughed, finishing their meal. Lily finally settled on a documentary about the Wild West and grinned slyly at her friend.

"I want to see what I missed when you went out there. Who knows, maybe it's time for me to trade my city life for a simpler one."

She winked at Serenity before bursting into laughter. Lily was a born-and-bred city girl who lived for parties, people, and fun. Serenity smiled, thinking about how her friend would react to the tiny town of Granite. It certainly didn't have the party scene of L.A., but it had its own special charm.

"You never know, it might be just what you need," she said, stirring her sticky rice and staring at the bottom of the container.

"What do you need, Ser?"

The serious tone of Lily's voice made Serenity glance at her friend.

"What do you mean?"

"I know you're not happy. I don't think you're pining over Chad. At least I certainly hope you're not. But ever since you got back, you haven't been your old self. I can't drag you out of here unless you're going to work. What's up?"

Serenity shrugged and focused on folding up her empty to-go containers before answering.

"I really can't explain it. Ever since I came back from that place, I've felt like I've been out of step. I just know something's missing, and I don't know how to fix it."

"I think it's time you finally come clean about that cowboy of yours," Lily said, fixing her friend with a serious look and shaking her finger at her. "And don't deny it."

Serenity's heart clenched, and she took a deep breath. Maybe telling someone about Austin would make it feel better. She'd refused to talk about her breakup with Chad, and Lily knew not to ask. She hadn't needed to. But she still had said little about her time at the ranch, preferring to hoard the memories to herself. She let out a sigh and started from the beginning.

"I guess you're right. We first met at the airport. He'd been sent to pick me up."

Serenity told her friend everything, and once she was done, she felt lighter. She glanced at the television screen and saw mountains that reminded her of the ones she'd recently left, and her heart clenched again.

"Wow, he sounds amazing. I know one thing: they don't grow men like that around here," Lily said. "What do you want to do about it?"

"What can I do? My life is here, not in the wilds of Wyoming. I have a career that most people would die to have, for Pete's sake. I'm leaving on an all-expense-paid trip to an idyllic resort in Iceland. I can't just walk away."

"Can't you?"

Serenity blinked hard and looked at her friend, half expecting to see a joking look on the redhead's face. Lily looked dead serious. She had her head cocked to the side, and she seemed earnest.

"Seriously? Like up and leave here and hope that Austin still remembers my name? No, I can't do that."

"I don't think he'd forget you. I think you two had a connection. From the sound of it, it sounds like it went both ways. If you want something, Ser, you've got to take it."

Serenity let out a shuddering sigh and leaned her head back against the couch.

"I wish I could, but it doesn't seem smart. It was just a few days. I can't jump and risk everything I've built on something that might not even be real. Heck, I bet he romances all the guests."

Lily made a face and shook her head.

"I don't think he's that kind of man. I won't tell you what to do, but think about it. Heck, everyone works from home these days. You could start your own travel blog. I could help you build your social following. You could even work remotely if that sounds too risky. You don't have to take these trips all the time, you know. Herm would give you another position in a heartbeat if you asked him. Just think about it."

Serenity looked out the window and nodded.

"I think it sounds insane. Thanks for talking me through it, though. In a perfect world, I might just make a leap like that, but right now, it sounds too risky. Someone else will come along."

"But will he be Austin?"

Tears sprang into Serenity's eyes, and she blinked them away. Why was she so hung up on him?

"No, he won't be Austin."

She gathered up their trash from the coffee table and

went into the kitchen. Lily followed and surprised Serenity by wrapping her in a hug.

"I just want you to be happy," she said, whispering into Serenity's hair. "I'm here for you, no matter what you choose."

"You're the best. I'm sorry to be such a downer. If it's okay with you, I'm going to go to bed."

Lily nodded and looped her arm through Serenity's.

"Absolutely. A good night's sleep is always important. I'm going to watch the rest of that documentary and see if I can spot any handsome cowboys. You never know; I may find one for myself someday."

"Good night, Lil. Thanks for everything."

Her friend waved her hand as they parted in the living room.

"I'd do anything for you. We're buds, remember? You've got my back, and I've got yours. Sleep well, okay? I'll keep the volume down."

Serenity walked over to the guest corner and sat on the bed, looking at her phone. She paged through the pictures she'd taken of the ranch before stopping at the one of the little cabin. She closed her eyes, remembering how it had felt to walk around the site and picture what the cabin would look like when it was finished. Her heart had felt like she'd finally come home when she was there. She turned off her phone and switched off the light, sinking back into the pillows, doing her best not to cry.

Chapter Sixteen

Austin

A strident car horn shocked him out of his stupor as he stared up at what had to be the tallest building he'd ever seen. A man bumped into his shoulder and kept going without a single glance back.

"Sorry," Austin said.

The man didn't even stop. Yep, he wasn't in Wyoming anymore; that was certain. He took a deep breath to steady himself and forced his boots to keep moving down the sidewalk.

The past three weeks had been pure torture. For the first time in his life, he hadn't been able to focus on his job. Unfortunately, for a ranch hand, that made getting hurt a real possibility. A horse had nearly kicked him in the head while he'd been daydreaming about Serenity's apple blossom scent and her eyes. He'd recovered and got the horse under control, but it had been a near thing.

Too near. He'd been called into Mr. Bohannon's office later that day. Austin shook his head, remembering the odd meeting and the questions Serenity had about his boss. When he'd first been hired, he'd written off Bohannon's peculiarities as just being eccentric, but now he was wondering.

At first, they'd talked about mundane things. He'd asked how Austin liked it at the ranch and where he saw himself in five years. Then the conversation had taken a strange turn. Austin flushed as he remembered what Bohannon had asked: What was the most important thing in Austin's life?

That question had thrown him for a loop, and it took him a few minutes to answer. The first image that popped into his mind was Serenity, sitting with him by a fire. If he closed his eyes, he could see her face, laughing with delight at one of his jokes, her dimple on full display, and the sad look in her eyes banished for good. He'd stopped mid-sentence, realizing that if he'd been asked that question a month ago, he would've had an entirely different answer.

Bohannon had been quiet for a minute before asking his last question. If he saw himself with the reporter, why not go after her? Why, indeed? Besides the fact that she was a city girl who lived in L.A., which was about as far away from Granite, Wyoming, as a person could get, would she even be interested in him? Could he really just show up and whisk her away?

His boss simply said, "Well, you'll never know till you ask her." Easy for him to say. Austin snorted as he found the building he was looking for. Bohannon had told him he had three days to get his hindquarters to L.A. and track Serenity down before he actually got his head kicked in. At least he'd know one way or another and could stop daydreaming and putting himself in risky situations.

It had taken Austin a split second to agree to Bohannon's terms. He remembered his boss chuckling and telling him to check the outbox on his desk. Right there, on the top, was an envelope with a plane ticket. He'd flown out that morning and arrived in Los Angeles just four hours later. His mind reeled as someone else shoved into him, going the other direction. The taxi ride here had been terrifying, and walking wasn't proving to be much better.

What kind of place was this? No one had the time to smile, let alone nod their head at you or even acknowledge your existence as a human being and not something standing between them and their destination? He couldn't imagine anyone finding happiness in a place like this, but from the multitude thronging around him, it was clear many people did.

He stopped at the building marked on his phone's GPS and looked upward. This was it. This was where *The Globe Trotter* had its offices. This was his moment of truth. He tapped his front pocket, feeling for the square box inside as if it were a lifeline. Questions swirled in his head as he walked in and looked for the building directory. He noticed a few people staring at him, and for the first time in his life, he felt self-conscious wearing a cowboy hat and boots. Was he about to make the biggest mistake of his life?

He finally found the listing for the magazine and whistled through his teeth. It was on the fortieth floor. He'd come this far, he thought, as he headed for the elevators. May as well keep going. He followed a group of people into the elevator and pressed his back against the wall. As the doors slid shut, he felt panic claw at his throat, and sweat started dripping down his back.

As the elevator lurched upward, he realized he'd forgotten to hit the button for his floor.

"Excuse me, ma'am," he said, touching the shoulder of the blonde woman in front of him.

"Oh. Oh my. Is there a movie filming here today?"

Austin cleared his throat, feeling very much like a tasty mouse who'd been cornered by a hungry cat.

"No, ma'am. Not that I'm aware of."

She turned towards him, nose flared, and looked him up and down. Her blonde hair looked like it had been shellacked into place so hard, he doubted if an F-5 tornado would move a strand.

"Well, I might arrange something if you'd like to star in a movie for me," she said.

Austin blushed, and the feeling of panic returned as he realized everyone in the elevator was staring at them.

"What floor, man?"

He glanced at the older gentleman standing near the buttons and nodded, grateful for the interruption.

"Forty, please."

"You got it."

The woman moved closer to him, and he could smell her perfume. It was a dark, heavy fragrance that made him feel even more claustrophobic.

"What do you say, cowboy? Want to take this city girl for a ride?"

The elevator dinged, and a few people got out, making the small space feel less crowded. The doors slid shut, and they lurched upward again.

"No, thank you, ma'am," Austin ground out from between his teeth.

"Well, if you change your mind, here's my card," she said, pressing it into his hand.

She turned back around and pressed close to him. He gulped and met the eyes of the man who'd helped him with the number. The man shook his head and shot Austin a wry grin.

The elevator stopped, and the woman in front of him finally moved forward and got out. As the doors slid shut, she winked and held up her fingers in the 'call me' gesture.

Just five more floors to go, Austin thought, resisting the urge to wipe his hands on his jeans. The doors opened, and he stepped out, gasping a little as he entered the wider hallway. He dropped the card the woman had given him into the trash can by the elevators and looked around. He spotted a woman down the hall and headed in her direction.

"Excuse me, ma'am. Do you know where Serenity Adams' office is?"

She looked at him blankly for a second before her mouth quirked into a smile.

"You must work for that one service, the singing telegram thing. Do they still do that? Serenity's gonna love this. She's been down for weeks. She's down the hall there and to the left. I've gotta go grab Gina. She won't want to miss this."

He tipped his hat and kept walking, mind racing faster than his feet could carry him. Serenity had been down too? Was it possible she'd missed him as much as he'd missed her? Maybe this crazy idea wasn't as crazy as he'd thought.

His heart filled with hope, and he said a quick prayer under his breath. The right words wouldn't come, but he supposed the good Lord heard the words 'help me' often enough to understand just what he needed.

He paused in front of the door with Serenity's name on it, paralyzed with indecision. Had he gone temporarily insane? Did he really expect this woman to leave all of this behind? She'd obviously worked very hard to get where she was, and now he expected her to let him carry her off to the middle of nowhere?

He'd almost turned around and slunk back to the ranch with his tail between his legs when the door flew open, and he got a quick glimpse of Serenity before she barreled right into him. He automatically put his arms around her to keep her from falling, and suddenly, everything felt right. Whatever it was he'd been missing for the past three weeks fell into place. He breathed in her sweet scent and closed his eyes. Her hand came up and squeezed his bicep, gripping him hard.

"Austin? Are you actually here? Have I finally lost it?"

He stepped back and looked into her eyes, heart thumping against his ribs.

"I'm really here."

He searched her face, feeling like a drowning man who'd been offered a yacht instead of a life jacket. She was even more beautiful than he remembered, but she still had that sad look in her eyes. There were little smudges of fatigue shadowing her face, and she looked thinner than the last time he'd seen her.

"I can't believe this. Why? How?"

He laughed and stepped towards her again, wanting to feel her in his arms. She rested her head on his chest and said something he couldn't quite hear.

"What was that?"

"I asked, why do I feel so right in your arms?"

His breath caught in his throat, and he found his courage. He stuck his hand in his pocket, took out the little box, and went down on one knee. She gasped as he opened it and looked into her face. The words he practiced on the plane ride here vanished, and instead, he spoke what came into his heart.

"Serenity Adams, I know we come from very different worlds. I know you could do so much better than a ranch hand like me. Despite that, all I know is my world isn't the same without you in it. Every moment since the day we met, you've been in my heart. You're the first thing I think about when I wake up, and your face is the last thing I see in my mind before I fall asleep. I may not have much, but I will work every single day of my life to become worthy of you. I will do everything in my power to make sure you never want for anything. I know it's sudden, insane, and unexpected, but I know I've met the love of my life, and I can't risk losing you. Would you do me the honor of becoming my wife?"

Chapter Seventeen

Serenity

The sound of two women gasping and dissolving into giggles yanked Serenity back into reality. She tore her eyes away from Austin, kneeling with the prettiest ring she'd ever seen, and frowned as she saw Gina and Stacy standing a few feet away.

"Is this all part of the act?" Gina asked in a loud whisper.

"Shhh, I don't know, but I don't want to miss anything," Stacy said in the same tone.

She looked back at Austin, still trying to make sense of what was happening. Had he really just proposed to her? She reached her hand out, desperate to get him off his knee and away from her co-workers.

"Let's go into my office," she said, pulling on his hand.

He followed her, clicking the box shut and shoving it in his pocket. She pushed the door shut and leaned against it, unsure of what had just happened. Her heart had been pounding ever since she laid eyes on Austin, and it kept hammering away as she thought about his words.

"I wasn't imagining that, right? You did just propose to me?"

Austin took his hat off and held it between his hands as he looked around her office before turning his intense gaze to her face.

"Yes, I did. If you don't feel the same way, I understand. I appreciate you taking me in here away from your friends before you answer."

She snorted and walked to the window, putting her hands on the sill and leaning on them, looking out but not seeing anything. Her pulse still thundered in her ears as she thought about his words. Marriage? Was it possible?

"Those two aren't my friends. I highly doubt they're anyone's friends, to be perfectly honest. I'm sorry our moment got interrupted."

She turned to face him, wanting to see the expression in his eyes before she spoke again.

"Austin, we barely..."

"Know each other. Yes, I'm aware of that. I also know that for the past three weeks, one day, and about eight hours, I've been thinking about you. I dang near got my head kicked in because I can't think about anything else. Gosh knows I've tried, but thinking about you has become as natural as breathing. Call me crazy, but I've never felt like this for anyone."

Tears welled in her eyes as he spoke. While she hadn't been in danger of being kicked in the head, she knew exactly what he'd been through. She'd experienced it firsthand. When she first saw him, she actually feared she was losing her mind and manifesting him in the hallway.

"I didn't say no, Austin," she said, her voice shaking. "I've thought about you, too. That's all I've done since I got back. I've thought about my life here, my future, and what I really want."

"And have you found any answers?"

She shook her head, wiping her tears away as they fell.

"I'm just so confused."

He walked toward her and held out his arms, welcoming her into his embrace. She stepped into his chest and closed her eyes, feeling like she'd come home. She couldn't explain it. Ever since she'd left the ranch, she'd felt like she was missing part of herself. Here, standing sheltered in Austin's muscular arms, she felt like she'd finally found it again.

"It's okay, Serenity," Austin said. "I'm confused, too. Maybe I jumped the gun, and for that, I'm sorry."

She shook her head and stepped back, trying to compose herself as she walked toward her desk and stacked papers mindlessly.

"How's everyone back at the ranch?"

"Dizzy sends her love. Shadow's growing like a little weed."

She tried to laugh, her voice breaking as she thought about the happy times she'd had on the ranch. If it hadn't been for Chad's ultimatum, she would've been tempted to extend her stay. Austin even remembered the name she'd given the kitten.

"I miss them so much. I missed you, Austin."

He took her hand in his, wrapping it securely.

"I suppose I should've asked if you'd patched things up with Chad before I barged in, talking about marriage."

She shook her head.

"No worries on that front. He called while I was still at the ranch to dump me and let me know I had three days to come get my things before he donated them to charity."

"What? Why didn't you tell me? Serenity, that's terrible. Where have you been staying?"

"It's fine. It was for the best. I found out he was cheating on me before he called, so it was definitely coming. I've been bunking with my friend Lily."

"Well, he's got to be the stupidest man on earth, that's all I have to say."

She looked into his eyes, surprised by the depth of feeling in them.

"Why?"

"If he was lucky enough to have you and threw it all away, he's obviously a blithering idiot."

His bald statement made her laugh, and she felt some of the tension in her chest ease.

"I appreciate that. You're the sweetest man I think I've ever met."

He pulled his head back and made a face that made her giggle.

"What?"

"I mean, I'll take sweet, but I'd prefer manly, strong, handsome..."

"You're all of those things, too," she said, stepping closer to him. "And many others."

He dipped his head lower and kissed her lips softly. She felt all of her cares melt away as the kiss deepened. If she'd thought his kiss when she left the ranch was amazing, this one put it to shame.

He stepped back, his blue eyes dark. Little jolts of lightning felt like they were tracing a path through Serenity's veins.

"I'd better stop before we go too far," he said, chest heaving.

She shuddered out a breath and nodded, crossing her arms over her chest. She felt cold outside of his embrace.

"Austin, what are we going to do? I want to say yes and go off with you, but..."

He slipped the box out of his pocket again and held it out.

"I might have spoken too soon, but my offer still stands. If you want to marry me today, tomorrow, or ten years from now, I'll wait for you. I don't have much, but everything I have is yours."

She opened the box, gasping now that she could focus on the ring. It was delicate, with vines that wound around its band, ending in flowers that held a beautiful diamond.

"Austin, it's perfect. How on earth?"

"I sold a few horses."

"Oh no, not Sally!"

Her eyes flew to his face, searching, and he chuckled as he stuck his hands in his pockets.

"Not Sally. I know you're partial to her. I had a few horses that were still on my brother's ranch. I know it's not a big rock, and you deserve so much more..."

She held up her hand to stop him.

"It's the most beautiful ring I've ever seen."

His handsome face relaxed, and that little muscle in his jaw stopped twitching as he smiled at her.

"I'm glad you like it. When I saw it, it reminded me of you."

She put the box on her desk, but her eyes kept going back to the ring, nestled in its little cushion. Lily had mentioned the possibility of her working from home. Could she really leave it all behind and go live with Austin in Wyoming? Where would they stay? It's not like she could share his bunk in the bunkhouse. Her savings account was tiny, but maybe she had enough to buy a little place in Granite. Indecision warred within her heart.

"How would it all work? I'm not lying when I say I want to be with you. More than anything. But how?"

"We'll figure it out, Serenity. I know you're used to the city and the finer things in life. You've been all over the world, and this is the first time I've been to California. We're complete opposites, but I know in my heart it will all work out if you want it to."

"I want it, Austin. More than you'll ever know. I want to just jump and say yes, but I'm afraid."

He nodded, his face serious as he looked at her.

"I'd be lying if I didn't admit that I'm over here, shaking in my boots. You don't have to answer me now. I know you have a lot to think about. Moving across the country doesn't happen overnight. I told you I'd wait for ten years, and I'd wait even longer than that if it meant a chance to have you in my life. Think about it. Decide what you want. I'll be waiting for you. Take all the time you need, Serenity. And if, well, if your answer is no, that's okay, too. All I want is for you to be happy. You know where to find me when you decide."

More tears welled in her eyes as his words hit home. The only other person who'd put her first like that had been her mother. A deep longing filled her heart as she wished desperately that her mother were still alive.

Austin came closer and put his finger under her chin, lifting her face up. Her breath caught in her chest as she saw the love he felt reflected in his eyes. He placed a kiss on her forehead and gave her a grin.

"We'll find a way. I promise you that. Keep the ring. It's yours, no matter what you decide."

"Austin..."

He picked up the box and pulled the ring out, placing it in her palm before gently folding her fingers over it.

"It's yours."

He turned to leave, boots rapping on the tile floor. It took her back to the moment they'd met at the airport.

She smiled at the memory and how she'd changed her mind about him since then.

"Where are you going?"

"Mr. Bohannon was nice enough to make this trip happen, but I should get back to work. I've got a return flight that's leaving in a few hours."

He paused, and the corner of his mouth came up.

"Yeah, I didn't really plan this out too well. All I knew was I had to see you. Hold you in my arms. Nothing else mattered. You've got my number, right?"

"I do. Thank you, Austin," she said, nodding as she gripped the ring in her hand. "I…"

"Just think about it, and when you're ready, let me know. Call me or text me whenever you want, day or night. I love you, Serenity Adams. I always will."

He tipped his hat to her, blue eyes sparkling, and walked out of her office. She stared at the door as it shut, mind racing.

Her heart screamed at her to follow him, join him on the flight, and leave without a second glance behind. Her head was currently speechless, lost in the logistics of what it would mean to leave everything behind and start her life over in the wilds of Wyoming.

She sank into her desk chair and put her head on the desk, still gripping the ring tightly in her hand. What did she really want? The past few weeks had taught her she wasn't happy, that she was missing something in her life, but was this the answer?

Serenity remembered the feeling she'd had when she was in Jim Bohannon's office and he'd prayed for her. It had been years since she'd prayed on her own, but right now, it seemed like the only thing she could do. She lifted her head and tried to think of the right words to say. Suddenly, they came out in a rush.

"God, I know it's been a long time since we've talked. I always used to pray back when my mom was alive, but once she passed, I got out of the habit, I guess. I don't know what to do, Lord. Please, guide my feet on the right path."

She trailed off and closed her eyes. The first thing that came to mind was Austin and how cherished he made her feel. Her life hadn't been the same since she'd left the ranch. It was almost like her eyes had been opened to the truth after years of being firmly closed. The life she thought she'd built was empty of meaning. All the things she thought she wanted made her feel like she was still missing something.

She opened her hand and looked at the ring, thinking about the man who'd given it to her. She slipped it on her ring finger, surprised that it fit like a glove. It felt right, and she never wanted to see another ring on that finger for the rest of her life.

Was that her answer? She nodded and reached for her phone, scrolling through the contacts until she found the right person.

"Herm? Do you mind if I come to your office? There are a few things we need to discuss?"

Chapter Eighteen

Austin

The hammer bounced painfully off his thumb, forcing a stifled yelp out of Austin as he shook his hand. Cooper, who'd somehow pulled building duty with him that day, laughed hard at his predicament, nearly falling off his perch on the truss of the cabin.

"What's that, the fifth time today?" Cooper asked, biting his lip as Austin glared at him.

"More like the fifth time this hour."

"Maybe you should stick to horses. I've only been up here a few times with you, and you keep getting injured every time."

"No kidding. I told Mr. Bohannon that, but he insisted I come up here again and help get these walls framed up. I guess the insulators and sheetrockers are coming tomorrow. He is in an all-fired hurry to get this place done. I wonder why?"

"Want to take a break?"

"I thought you'd never ask," Cooper said, giving Austin a grin as he swung down like a monkey.

Austin took the ladder, preferring not to take any more risks. While he loved horses, he appreciated the challenge that building the cabin brought. And the distraction. As long as he was making sure everything was level and sturdy, he wasn't thinking about Serenity. Much.

He joined Cooper on the porch and sat down on the steps, looking out over the prairie to the mountains in the distance.

"What do you think the boss intends to do with this place?" Cooper asked, reaching into the lunchbox he had stowed by the door.

"I'd guess it's going to be a guest cabin. Once we're done with the interior, we're supposed to build a fence around the place. It'll be nice once it's done."

"I could handle living in a place like this," Cooper said, biting into an apple.

"You had lunch not more than an hour and a half ago."

"A tough man like me needs a lot of fuel. Any luck on finding a place in town?"

Austin snorted and leaned against the porch railing.

"Not a thing."

Ever since he'd gotten back two weeks ago, he'd focused on finding a place he could share with Serenity. They talked on the phone every night, and Austin hated reporting that once again, he'd come up empty. There was no way they could stay in the bunkhouse together. She'd assured him it didn't matter, and they'd figure it out, but he wanted to provide for her.

"You'll find something. I know Granite's a small town, but you'd think someone would have a house for sale or even rent. Heck, you've gotten some experience with building thanks to this little place. Maybe you could build a new house."

Austin snorted again and closed his eyes. He was running out of time to figure it out.

"If that's what has to happen, I'd build it all with my two hands, but I still have to work. Now that we've got guests coming and going, I'm going to be needed for the trail rides and lessons the boss wants me to give new riders. Serenity's figuring out a remote work contract, but I'm not gonna have her build our house. She deserves a nice house. She already gave up the trip of a lifetime to Iceland. I can't ask her to keep giving things up for me."

"Maybe we could partition off a room in the bunkhouse," Cooper said, tossing his apple core into the yard.

"That's possibly the least romantic thing I could ever imagine."

Cooper rooted around in his lunch box and made a face when he came up empty. Austin shook his head and got to his feet.

"Well, sitting here won't get this cabin built. We've only got two more walls to go, and we can call it off for the day and get you some more food."

Cooper's stomach rumbled loudly, forcing Austin to laugh.

"Sounds good to me."

They went back inside, and Austin tried to forget about his problems as they finished up their work for the day. He'd asked Cassie for help in finding a place, figuring she knew everyone in town, but even she had come up empty. Unless someone moved away in the next few weeks, he had no choice but to admit failure.

His job at the ranch meant commuting from nearby Jackson would be difficult, let alone the fact that a ranch hand couldn't exactly afford a place in that ritzy town. As he packed up their tools for the day, he thought about other options. A camper? No, he thought, shaking his head. He couldn't ask Serenity to live in a camper. She was used to life in a big city and traveling to exclusive resorts.

Cooper walked up behind him and clapped his hand on Austin's shoulder.

"Don't sweat it, man. Something will come up."

"From your lips to God's ear. Let's head back. With any luck, Martha will have dinner ready so you don't pass out from hunger."

Cooper gave him a thumbs-up as he jumped in the passenger side and cranked up the tunes. The ride back to the ranch was punctuated with Cooper's shouting to the music. While he lacked musical ability, he sure made up for it with enthusiasm. Austin waited to turn off the pickup until Cooper finished the last words of a song.

"You couldn't carry a tune in a bucket, you know that?"

"Hey, that's some fine singing, if I say so myself," Cooper answered, smiling as he slammed the door shut. "Maybe you need to adjust your ears."

Austin chuckled as he followed Cooper up the steps to the ranch house. As soon as they opened the door, Cooper sniffed deeply.

"I think it's pot roast night."

"That's what we're having, and you keep your mitts to yourself if you know what's good for you," Martha said, appearing from the kitchen. "We'll be eating in half an hour. If you're hungry—and I'm guessing you are—there's some bread on the counter. You get one piece. One!"

"Thanks, Miss Martha," Cooper said, heading for the kitchen.

"Austin, Mr. Bohannon asked if you'd join him in his office."

"Did he say what it was about?" Austin asked as he walked to the stairs.

"No, he didn't. Get your hind end up there, and you'll find out for yourself," Martha said. "And when you get back, you can put your dish-stacking skills to good use and help me get the table ready. We've got a special guest tonight."

Austin stopped halfway up the stairs and looked back at Martha.

"Really? Is it a VIP guest?"

She smiled and shrugged, disappearing into the kitchen and shouting at Cooper to put down a roll.

Austin jogged up the remaining steps and went down the hall to the office. Even though he had done nothing wrong, he still felt a qualm of anxiety stir in his stomach. He shook his head, recalling how it felt to be called into the principal's office at school. He rapped on the door and heard Bohannon's voice through the thick door.

"Enter."

He walked into the room and saw his boss wasn't alone. There was a woman sitting in a chair across from the desk. Something about her hair was familiar, and as he walked closer, his heart started pounding. The scent of apple blossoms reached his nose, and he walked faster.

"Serenity?"

She jumped out of the chair and closed the distance, burying her face in his chest. He wrapped his arms around her before remembering he'd been working all day and sweating like a prize racehorse. He tried to take a step back.

"Serenity, wait, I haven't showered, and I've been working all day. I probably stink to high heaven."

"I don't care," she said, her voice muffled by his shirt. "I've missed you so much."

"Good to see you, Austin. I gather you're happy about this surprise."

Jim Bohannon smiled at them, and for a second, Austin thought he reminded him of someone else, but that thought careened off as Serenity kissed his cheek.

"I couldn't be any happier. How did you get here? We just talked last night. I thought you were in California."

She stepped back, eyes glowing.

"I wanted to surprise you. I got everything wrapped up, and Mr. Bohannon called me and offered to fly me out. I hope it's okay that I'm here earlier than we planned."

"Okay? It's more than okay," he said, taking her in his arms again, unable to believe she was really here. "There's just one problem."

"I think I have the answer to that problem," Jim said. "Take a seat, Austin."

Austin held Serenity's hand as they sat back down. He kept glancing over at her, sure this was all a dream, but she was really there.

"On my desk, you'll see an envelope. Austin, please open it and see what you think."

Austin and Serenity looked at each other as he grabbed the envelope and tore it open. His heart stuttered in his chest as he realized he was holding a deed of some sort.

"I don't understand," Serenity said, looking into Austin's eyes.

He looked into her soft brown eyes and felt his heart turn over at the love he saw reflected in their depths. He went back to the paper and started reading.

"I signed over the deed for the cabin and a few acres of land to the two of you," Bohannon said.

Austin's mouth fell open, and he looked at Bohannon's back in disbelief.

"Sir?"

"I know it's not done yet, but Serenity, you're more than welcome to stay here in the Canyon Room again until the cabin is complete. It should only take a few weeks to get it finished, and of course, you can help pick the finishes to make it yours. If you don't like it…"

"Oh, Mr. Bohannon, I love it," Serenity said, glancing at Austin with tears in her eyes. "When I saw the place, my first thought was that I would love to live in a little cabin like that."

Austin reached his hand up to Serenity's face and wiped away a tear with his thumb.

"Sir, I don't know what to say. I'd be happy to pay for the place. There's no way I could buy it up front, but maybe you'd take payments out of my salary."

"Nonsense, son. I have more money than I know what to do with and plenty of land. Think of it as an early wedding present. You'll also notice the deed doesn't specify that you have to remain in my employ. The place belongs to both of you, no strings attached."

Austin's heart swelled, and he felt tears prick the back of his eyes. His own father hadn't treated him like this, and he wasn't sure what to say.

"It's too much," he said, clearing his throat.

"It's not enough. You're an outstanding employee, Austin. Serenity has helped me more than you know with your glowing write-up on the place. We'll have more guests than we know what to do with. Please, accept it with my humble thanks."

Austin looked over at Serenity, and she nodded at him, smiling gently. This meant they would have the chance to start their life together in their own place, on their own land. It was more than he thought he'd ever had.

"Thank you, sir. I'll do everything in my power to be worthy of a gift like this."

"You already are. You both are. Serenity, I'd also like to offer the ranch as a site for your future wedding, whenever that may be. You don't have to have it here, but I know the preacher in town would be happy to come out and officiate. Just say the word and I'll make it happen."

"Oh, that would be the most wonderful thing," Serenity said, looking at Austin. "We haven't set a date."

"Tomorrow would be good," Austin said, winking at her and holding her hand a little tighter.

They laughed, and Serenity nodded.

"We don't want to wait," she said. "The sooner, the better."

"Excellent. Leave everything to me, and I'll get everything organized. Do you have any guests you'd like to invite?"

Serenity thought about it, but other than Lily, there wasn't anyone she'd want to join them on their special day.

"Just one person. That's all I have," she said.

Austin's heart tightened.

"You've got Martha, me, and all the other cowboys here. We'll make sure it's an event to remember," he said, itching to hold her close. "We'll have to get you a dress."

Jim Bohannon cleared his throat.

"Don't worry about anything. I'll make sure you have everything you need."

"You don't have to do that," Serenity said. "I have a little savings I can use."

"Please, humor me. I, well, I have no children, and this is something I'd like to do for you both. Now, if you'll excuse me, I've got a wedding to plan," Bohannon said with a laugh. "You two go have some supper. I have a feeling you have some catching up to do. I'll send down some samples so you can pick the interior of your new home. Austin, you'll have to take her up to see the place so she can get some ideas."

Austin nodded and stood, holding onto Serenity's hand like a lifeline.

"I'll do that. Thank you, sir."

He led Serenity out of the office, convinced he was about to wake up from a dream, but as they entered the hall, it hit him that all of their prayers were answered.

"Austin, do you think Mr. Bohannon is an angel?" Serenity asked, stopping him in his tracks.

"I was just thinking that all of our prayers were answered in one fell swoop. They say the Lord moves in mysterious ways, so you might just be right."

They walked down the stairs, hand in hand. Austin glanced at her profile, his heart rising in his chest as he thanked God for her.

"Do we have time to see Dizzy, Shadow, and the horses before we eat?" Serenity asked.

He glanced down at the table, seeing it was still empty.

"Tell you what. Help me get the table set, and we'll make time."

"Race you!"

She laughed as she released his hand and raced down the stairs, intent on seeing her furry friends. He watched her run, hair swinging, and thought about how much they'd both changed since the day they met. She seemed truly happy. As he started down the stairs, he promised himself that he'd do everything he could to ensure she stayed that way.

Epilogue

Gus

Gus leaned against the windowsill, watching as the guests filtered in for the wedding in the garden. Even though he'd never had children, he felt like a proud parent as the seats filled in. The garden had been completely transformed for the event, and for once, it looked as though the weather was going to cooperate.

The guests' laughter filtered up through the house, and he smiled. Even though he wouldn't be present for the event, it was enough to observe and thank God that everything had gone to plan. In fact, Gus thought, with a chuckle, it had far exceeded any of his plans. He didn't know from the start that Serenity and Austin would click like they had, that they would want to be married as soon as possible, but here they were.

The finishing touches were going on at the little

cabin he'd given the couple, and by the time they got back from their honeymoon, everything would be ready. He eased back from the window and nodded, content that he'd done everything he could to make today a happy one for Austin and Serenity.

A sharp rap on the door startled him.

"Enter."

"There you are, you old coot," Herman Thompson said before pulling the door shut behind him. "You don't have to hide up here, you know."

Gus smirked at his old friend and leaned forward.

"You know how I feel about getting recognized, Herm. Today's about those kids down there, not me. Glad you could make it."

Herm sat across from the desk with a groan and tapped his fingers on the edge of it.

"I could hardly turn down the free ticket that popped into my email, now could I? You said you wanted to talk to me about something when I got here?"

Gus leaned back in his chair, steepling his fingers over his middle as he thought about the last few things he wanted to do for Serenity. The woman had touched him with her bravely hidden vulnerability, and he'd hoped he could make this day a happy one for her. He knew her mother had passed years ago, and she'd never mentioned her father. The only person she seemed close to, other than Austin and her friend Lily, was this man, her editor.

"How do you feel about giving Serenity away?"

Herm cocked an eyebrow and shook his head.

"Are you serious?"

Gus nodded, glancing towards the window as more laughter sounded below. He focused back on his friend.

"I am. She hasn't said anything, but I know something's been wearing on her. I think that's part of it. You don't have to do it if it makes you uncomfortable."

Herm waved off his words and nodded slowly.

"I'll do it. It's the least I can do. Serenity's always gone above and beyond for me. I'm going to miss having her around the office. She may turn me down, but I'll offer. I'll admit, when you told me about your crazy, half-baked plan, I thought you'd finally lost it."

Gus snorted and shook his head.

"I probably have lost it. To be honest, I didn't think it would work either. It just popped into my head, and I went with it."

Herm leaned forward, eyes twinkling.

"What else do you have up your sleeve, you old coot?"

"I've got some ideas in the works. We just got a new booking for a week from now, and something spoke to me. A vegetarian chef is coming to stay. I did a little digging, and it looks like she's out of work. I could use someone like that to help Martha out in the kitchen."

"A vegetarian chef on a cattle ranch? Isn't that, well, pardon the pun, a recipe for failure?"

"You might be surprised. We've got people calling from all over the world, thanks to that piece Serenity did for your rag. We need to be able to keep up with the times. I won't judge people who want to eat in a certain way. Martha's a marvel in the kitchen, but with the ranch taking off, she can't do it all."

Herm slapped his knee and laughed, shaking his head.

"Leave it to you to come up with something crazy like that. I'd like to hear how it turns out. How are things, by the way, Gus? Or should I say Jim Bohannon?"

Gus tightened his shoulders and eased back in his chair. He'd known Herm for twenty years at least. They'd met when Herm was a reporter in California, covering rodeos. Who would have thought his old friend would end up running a premier travel magazine? Life was crazy, that was for sure.

"You know how I feel about my privacy. I don't want sympathy, or God forbid, pity. I just want to do what I can and help people. It's easier if they don't know who I am."

"Don't worry, I won't blow your cover. It's interesting, is all. You know Serenity's one smart cookie, right? Sooner or later, she's going to figure it out."

"Well, hopefully it will be later. That was nice of you to let her have a few weeks off for her honeymoon."

Herm smiled, his familiar cat-got-the-canary grin, and his eyes wrinkled in the corners.

"I'm doing one better than that. Serenity was supposed to be covering a resort in Iceland instead of getting married. I know how much she was looking forward to that trip. I reorganized a few things and got her two tickets and all accommodations paid. She just needs to write a piece on it when she comes back."

Gus's heart swelled at the generosity of his old friend. He'd wanted to do something similar for the couple, but Austin had put his foot down, stating the wedding, cabin, and everything else were more than enough. Now, thanks to Herm, the couple would have an all-star honeymoon as well.

"Do they know yet?"

Herm stood, straightening the cuffs of his shirt.

"Not yet, but I'm about to tell them. Are you sure you won't join me? You don't have to hide up here. It's been two decades at least. Chances are, everyone here would be too young to remember your bull riding days."

Gus's face tightened, and he felt that familiar panic claw at his throat as he shook his head.

"No."

Herm heaved a sigh.

"All right then. I'll stop back up here before I leave. Maybe we can have a few drinks and toast to the old days."

"I'd like that."

Herm left, and Gus slowly stood, walking over to the window again. Austin had taken his place near the preacher at the fountain, and the band was tuning up. His heart caught in his throat as he suddenly thought of Rose. He'd always imagined what it would be like to stand next to the preacher and see her walk down an aisle toward him.

He wondered where Rose was today. Had she married? Had children? Even though he had the best private investigators at his fingertips, he'd never looked into her. Some things were better not knowing. He shook off his melancholy and focused his attention back on the garden. Austin looked happy as he stood, waiting for Serenity, laser-focused on the back of the house where she'd appear.

Gus looked at his ranch hands, lined up in the front row. Jack was, predictably, keeping to himself, arms crossed across his chest. Gus bit his lip, considering what could be done for the cowboy. He'd been in those shoes and knew how hard it was to fight an addiction. He also knew that until Jack was ready, any efforts to help him might not work. Something needed to be done, soon, though.

He watched as Cooper popped up and jogged over to Austin, whispering something in his ear that made him laugh and relax his shoulders. Cooper was always the life of every party, ready with a joke and a laugh. He looked down the rest of the row, thinking about the future, but his eyes kept going back to Cooper. Which cowboy could he help next?

The musicians started up the Wedding March, interrupting his thoughts. He felt his eyes fill with tears as he watched Serenity walk down the aisle on Herm's arm. She'd agreed then. He nodded sharply and cleared his throat, trying to keep his emotions in check. He could just make out Serenity's face as she came to a stop in front of Austin. She looked radiant as she gazed at the cowboy as the ceremony began.

Gus stayed at the window, watching as they exchanged vows and then rings. Once the happy couple walked back down the aisle, he returned to his desk, overcome with emotion. He bowed his head as he sat and tried to come up with the right words.

"God, Father in Heaven, thank You for bringing

these two together. I ask for Your help to continue my efforts to help people find love and healing. I know it's too late for me, and I made the wrong choices in my life, but with Your help, we can make a difference in so many lives. Please, continue to work through me."

He trailed off and wiped the tears that continued to stream down his cheeks. He glanced at the list of his hired hands, once again focusing on Cooper's name. Maybe it was time for the Montana cowboy to meet his match. He'd have to see how everything played out.

Gus leaned back in his chair, content to dream about the future as he listened to the merriment continue below. Visions of Rose worked their way into his head as he nodded off, and a smile stole across his face, relaxing the harsh lines. He sighed as he fell asleep, dreaming of his lost love.

A Note From Casey

Thank you for taking the time to read this novel. If you enjoyed the book, please take a few minutes to leave a review. As an independent author, I appreciate the help!

If you'd like to be first in line to hear about new books as they are released, don't forget to sign up for my newsletter. Click here - http://www.booksbycasey.com/sign-up-to-my-free-newsletter/

Missing The Mended Hearts Ranch already?

The Mended Hearts Ranch, Book 2 - Finding Fiona

A Heartwarming Women's Fiction Novel. Coming Soon!

Fiona Harper has always known who she is, or at least, she thought she did.

A talented chef with a thriving career and a future she believed was secure, Fiona's world shatters when a sudden betrayal costs her both her relationship and the work she poured her heart into. With her confidence shaken and her sense of identity in pieces, she leaves everything behind and heads west, unsure of what comes next.

The Mended Hearts Ranch offers Fiona more than a place to stay. It gives her time to breathe, hands-on work that feels meaningful, and a community that quietly reminds her of her own worth. As she begins cooking again, not for recognition or ambition, but for the simple joy of it, Fiona starts to rediscover the woman she used to be.

Yet rebuilding a life is never as simple as starting over. Old fears linger, and trusting her instincts again feels like the hardest step of all. When a someone challenges the walls she's carefully rebuilt, Fiona must decide whether she's ready to believe in herself, and in the possibility of something more.

Finding Fiona is a heartwarming story about resilience, self-discovery, and learning that sometimes the bravest thing you can do is claim your life back on your own terms.